FIELD TRIPPED

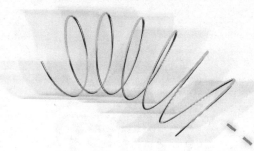

ALSO BY ALLAN WOODROW

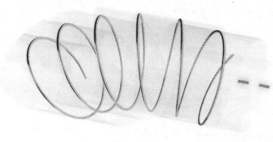

FIELD TRIPPED

ALLAN WOODROW

SCHOLASTIC PRESS | NEW YORK

J

Library of Congress Cataloging-in-Publication Data

Names: Woodrow, Allan, author
Title: Field tripped / Allan Woodrow.
Description: First edition. | New York : Scholastic Press, 2018. | Summary: The fifth graders of Liberty Falls Elementary have a reputation for trouble, but they still have a field trip to the mansion of Edward Minks (local inventor, founder of the town, and great-great-great grandfather of fifth-grader Eddie). While there, they search for secret inventions that are rumored to be hidden in the mansion—but they find that they are not the only ones searching, and somehow this class of trouble-makers must work together to thwart the thieves.
Identifiers: LCCN 2017055136 | ISBN 9781338116915
Subjects: LCSH: School field trips—Juvenile fiction. | Inventors—Juvenile fiction. | Inventions—Juvenile fiction. | Secrecy—Juvenile fiction. | Theft—Juvenile fiction. | CYAC: School field trips—Fiction. | Inventors—Fiction. | Inventions—Fiction. | Secrets—Fiction. | Stealing—Fiction.
Classification: LCC PZ7.W86047 Fi 2018 | DDC 813.6 [Fic]—dc23

10 9 8 7 6 5 4 3 2 1   18 19 20 21 22

Printed in the U.S.A.   23
First edition, September 2018

Book design by Yaffa Jaskoll

To those who have dared—dared to reach, dared to dream—and who have illuminated us and inspired us through their perseverance and genius. Also, this book is dedicated to pickles.

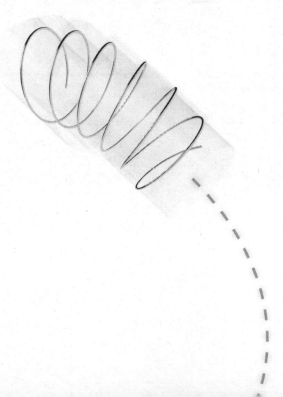

1
AARON

I sit straight at my desk while everyone else in class buzzes about the field trip. We're going to a crazy mansion built by a guy who founded our town *and* invented more than two thousand things, including a hundred things that have something to do with pickles.

Also, the place may be haunted, but maybe not. At least that's what I overheard kids say during lunch.

There isn't anything to do when you sit by yourself at lunch other than overhear kids talking. My family moved here a couple months ago from Alaska. I sat by myself at lunch for a long time there, too. But then I made friends.

It's hard to make new friends when you move a lot. But it's easy to overhear stuff.

I'm sitting here by myself in class, too, waiting to leave on the trip. We'll be gone all afternoon and back before dinner. Just about everybody seems to be bouncing in their seats.

"Can you believe we're finally going?" asks Chloe. She sits behind me in class.

I turn to answer her, but she's not talking to me. She's talking to her friend Sophie.

"Whatever," Sophie says to Chloe, shrugging.

Sophie doesn't seem too thrilled about this trip, but I think she's the only one. Two of the four Liberty Falls fifth-grade classes are going. The other two classes in our grade go next week.

While the rest of the class whispers and bounces, I slip Dad's letter from my notebook. I got it yesterday. It starts:

Atten-shun, Private Wharton!

That's what Dad writes at the top of each of his letters to me. It's sort of a joke. When I was a little squirt, a kindergarten-little squirt, I liked to pretend I was in the army so I could be more like Dad.

I always sign my letters to him the same way: *Private Aaron Wharton.*

Dad always ends his letters one way, too:

Over and Out, First Sergeant Wharton

P.S. Serve. Protect. Be all you can be.

I try to be all I can be, but I'm not sure if I even know what I can be yet.

Mrs. Greeley, our teacher, clears her throat. Then she coughs a few times. She's been coughing all morning. I slide the letter back into my notebook. "Is everyone ready?" she asks before coughing again.

A big cheer fills the room. This trip will be awesome—but I'm sure I'd have more fun if I was going with my last class, the one in Alaska. I miss my house, my room, my backyard, our army base's dog, and the big tree I liked to climb with the tree house that I never finished. I miss everything but the weather. It's cold here, but it was even colder in Alaska.

Maybe next time Dad will be sent somewhere warmer. Or, better yet, maybe we won't go anywhere else. I'm tired of moving all the time and not fitting in.

It's extra hard to fit in when you're not sure how you're supposed to fit. When you live somewhere for a while, you just sort of know that stuff. I don't even look like I fit in anywhere. My skin isn't quite dark like Dad's but not quite light like Mom's, and my hair is not quite curly but not quite straight. I'm stuck in the middle of Mom and Dad, just like I'm stuck sitting by myself at lunch.

Dad says everyone fits in somewhere. He says I just need to find my somewhere.

"As many of you already know," says Mrs. Greeley, "the Minks Mystery Mansion was the home of Edward Minks IV, also known as the Innovator of Invention, the General of Genius, or most commonly, *the Legend of Liberty Falls*! He not only founded our town, but some say he was the world's greatest inventor, or maybe the world's second-greatest inventor. Top three for sure. Depends on the list."

"Did you know that he invented the school bell?" asks Eddie. He blurts it out without raising his hand. "Before that, kids never left class because no one knew school ended."

"He invented the school bell as we know it today," says Mrs. Greeley. "But bells have been around thousands of years and so have schools. I'm sure they always had ways to end classes."

Eddie shakes his head. He adjusts his glasses. He leans back and crosses his arms. "No, I am quite sure that kids never left school, even for summer vacation. That's why his invention was so important." When he talks, he lifts his chin, and sort of acts like he knows more than our teacher or anyone.

Mrs. Greeley smiles, but she's got this look on her face like she's trying extra hard to keep her smile but doesn't quite feel like smiling.

Everyone sort of has a hard time keeping a smile around Eddie. At lunch he sits at a table with a whole bunch of other kids, but he sits at the end and no one pays attention to him. When they do, they sort of frown.

I'd rather sit by myself at lunch than have everyone at my table frown at me.

I guess Eddie doesn't really fit in anywhere, either.

Last week it was a big surprise when Mrs. Greeley told us that Edward Minks was Eddie's great-great-great-grandfather. Eddie didn't look happy that she told our class. I think he wanted to keep it a secret, but I don't know why. If I were the ancestor of someone famous, I'd want everyone to know.

"The Minks Mansion is very big," says Mrs. Greeley. "When the main house was first built, there were forty-two rooms, but the house grew and grew, and now it has one hundred and twenty-four rooms, including thirty-eight bedrooms. There are staircases that rise up to nowhere, doors that open into walls and others that open into thin air."

"Why did he build such a strange house?" asks Chloe. She smiles. Chloe has the biggest, friendliest smile in class. Her green eyes get all bright and shiny.

"Because Minks was a weirdo," says Sophie with an eye roll. She sort of smiles, too, but she has the unfriendliest smile in class.

"He was not a weirdo," says Eddie, still crossing his arms. "He was brilliant."

"I heard some people called him the Loony Bird of Liberty Falls," says Sophie.

"People just didn't understand his genius," grunts Eddie.

"Let's just say he was a bit eccentric," says Mrs. Greeley.

I nod, but *eccentric* is just a nicer word for *weirdo*.

"Some say there are rooms that have never been found," says our teacher. "And that one of those rooms is filled with secret inventions the Legend of Liberty Falls never told anyone about."

"Like what?" Chloe asks.

Mrs. Greeley shrugs. "That's why they call it the Minks Mystery Mansion. But they say the Mysterious Machines of Mr. Minks would be worth a fortune if they existed." Then she coughs a whole bunch of times.

"Maybe he invented a cow," says Chloe. "But instead of giving milk it gives cookies. And then you get a regular cow and you can have milk and cookies every night."

"Or maybe he invented a chocolate milk cow," says Sophie. "Because regular milk is dumb."

Chloe's big smile fades a little.

"There is no secret room," says Eddie. He speaks loudly and puffs out his cheeks. "People have looked for that room for years. If there were a room, it would have been found already."

"You never know," says Mrs. Greeley. "Anyway, it's time to go." She turns and coughs. And coughs. And coughs. Her face looks as white as her hair, and Mrs. Greeley has very white hair.

While she clears her throat, I snag my backpack from beneath my seat and get in line.

I hope the trip is fun. I hope I fit in. Maybe I'll even make a friend.

Now, that would be one perfect invention—an automatic friend-maker.

"This will be the best trip ever," says Chloe, standing behind me and talking to Sophie. "Imagine if we found those secret inventions! Wouldn't that be funtastic?"

"Whatever," says Sophie, fixing her hair while looking at her reflection in the door window.

"I'm telling you, there are no inventions," says Eddie. He looks away when he says that. Sometimes, people look away when they aren't telling the whole truth.

Dad gave me the same look when I asked if his army unit was being deployed again and if he had to leave. He looked away and said he wasn't leaving, but the next week he was gone.

2

JESSIE

As we stand in line to walk to the bus, kids talk about what sort of inventions might be hidden in the house. Norm, a big kid with more freckles than you can count, says, "I bet he invented a burp pill, and if you ate it, your burps would smell like bananas."

"That's gross," says Sophie.

Norm blinks at her. "Why? I like bananas."

"There are no secret inventions," growls Eddie, stomping his foot. He looks angry.

I pull my backpack tighter around my shoulders. I love my backpack. It's brown with ears at the top so it looks like a cat. There's a special button on the strap. When I squeeze it, it squeals, *Meow!*

"Jessie Wang—did you bring a cat?" Mrs. Greeley asks sternly.

"That was just my backpack," I say.

"Good. I don't think the mansion staff would appreciate animals running around."

Then I follow Mrs. Greeley and the rest of our class down the hallway.

If Mr. Minks has a secret invention, I hope it's a cat groomer. My cats have to lick their fur all the time, and their tongues must get tired.

We have three cats at home. Mama says that cats have a special place in Chinese history. She says, according to old stories, you can tell time by looking into a cat's eyes. I've tried that, but all I see are cat eyeballs. So I'm pretty sure those stories are wrong.

I follow my class down the hall. A few kids are home sick today, including my best friend, Vivian. When I talked to Viv last night, she said she felt miserable and that she wouldn't be here today.

I press my backpack.

Meow!

I miss Vivian, but my backpack cheers me up.

We walk out the school doors. It's cold today. Last week it was warm. I wish the weather would just make up its mind what it wants to be. At least I wore my winter jacket and gloves.

A bus waits for us next to the curb. Mrs. Rosenbloom's class already stands in front of it, along with Principal Klein.

He wears a bright orange winter coat. It's the same color orange as the cardigan sweaters he always wears. He reminds me a little of Patches, my tabby cat. Tabby cats are orange, too.

In front of me, Mrs. Greeley coughs loudly. She's been coughing all morning.

"Dear me!" exclaims Principal Klein.

"I don't feel very well," says Mrs. Greeley.

"Maybe you should go home," Principal Klein says. "There are nasty bugs going around. You don't want to give anything to the kids."

"But what about the trip?" asks Mrs. Greeley, but it comes out more like "But what about . . . cough, cough . . . the . . . cough, cough . . . trip?"

"I'll be happy to go in your place," Principal Klein says. "I love the Minks Mystery Mansion! Besides, our fifth graders are very responsible. It'll be fun! Go home. Rest. And drink plenty of fluids and chicken soup."

"Thank you. I suppose I should," Mrs. Greeley answers, and then coughs about twenty times.

As our teacher staggers back into the school, still coughing, Principal Klein claps his hands. "Listen up, fifth graders." Principal Klein's voice booms. In assemblies, he doesn't even need a microphone. "I'm afraid Mrs. Greeley is going to miss our field trip. But I'm going instead—and I know we'll have a splendid time. The Minks Mystery Mansion is a magical place, full of wonders and secrets and pickles. And who doesn't love pickles? I expect each and every one of you to be on your very best behavior."

"We'll be the best-behaved class ever," says Sophie.

"That's wonderful to hear," says Principal Klein, smiling at Sophie.

I shake my head. Sophie is all smiles and curtsies with adults and teachers, but she's a different Sophie, a much meaner Sophie, when adults aren't around.

My cats wouldn't like Sophie. My cats have excellent taste.

Our principal spreads his arms. He has very large hands. "Don't forget, you all will need to write an essay about what you learn today. It's due next week."

Norm calls out, "Is there really a room filled with secret inventions?"

Principal Klein chuckles. "That's just an old rumor."

"But what if there is?" Norm asks. "If I find a secret invention room, will I get an A-plus on my essay?"

Principal Klein chuckles again. "That sounds fair. If anyone finds a secret invention room, he or she will automatically get an A-plus."

It would be simply incredible to find a room of hidden inventions, and Mama and Papa would love my getting an A-plus. But I'm sure Principal Klein is right and it's just a rumor. Too bad.

A gloomy breeze blows through us and the clouds look gray. Mrs. Rosenbloom, standing near me, frowns. She wraps her arms around herself because her jacket isn't as warm as mine.

"I hear a horrible snowstorm is brewing," says Mrs. Rosenbloom.

Principal Klein nods. "Strange weather we're having. But the reports say the storm should miss us." Then he announces, "Everyone on the buses."

As I walk up the bus steps, another strong breeze blows against my back. I shiver a little. The clouds don't seem as far away as they did this morning. I wish my cats were here to protect me.

I'm much braver when I'm with my cats, and it's hard to act brave when the sky looks so scary.

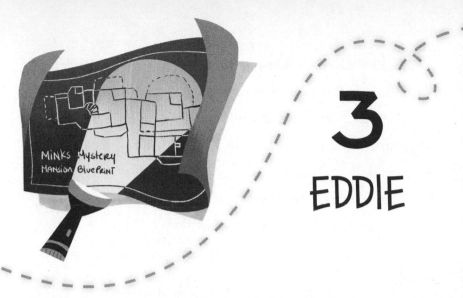

3
EDDIE

I spy an empty seat near the back of the bus. I toss my back-pack on it and then slide in.

No one sits next to me. No one will sit by me. They know it. I know it.

Just as well.

I have things to do.

"I bet one of the secret inventions is a machine that makes gold," says Seth. He's in Mrs. Rosenbloom's class and sits next to Brian. They are the biggest bullies in our grade. They're big, but not so smart.

I'm smart, but not so big. Or at least I'm not so tall. Mom says I'm shaped like my dad. That just means we're both a little round.

Mom also says I'll grow taller someday, as tall as Dad, but Mom says a lot of things and they aren't always true. For instance, she says I don't need a new backpack, even though

I've used the same one since second grade and it has choo-choo trains all over it. She says it's not a big deal that Dad's out of work. She says it's wonderful that my great-great-great-grandfather gave all of his money to charities and stuff.

"Out of what?" asks Brian.

"What out of what?" asks Seth.

"The secret invention that makes gold. It makes gold out of what?"

"Silver. It makes gold from silver."

"Oh. That makes sense."

No it doesn't. It makes absolutely no sense. I should just let them talk about things that make no sense. But I know they are wrong and I have a hard time keeping quiet around people that make no sense.

"There is no invention that makes gold," I say. Then I add, "There is no secret invention room or any hidden inventions at all. Everyone knows that."

But that is not true. Or at least I don't think it is true.

When he died, my great-great-great-grandfather left everything to Liberty Falls: his house, his inventions, and all his money, except—

Except he left a will, and at the end of his will, he wrote:

And to my children and their children and their children and so on—I leave my legacy and my secrets.

Secrets! Why would he write he was leaving secrets if he didn't have any to leave? That would make no sense. And if those secrets are hidden inventions, I'll be the one to find them.

"Eddie, you must go to the mansion pretty often, right?" asks Chloe. She sits across from me, one row up. "Since you're related to the inventor and all."

"Every week," I say.

Actually, I have never been to the Minks Mystery Mansion. It costs ten dollars to get in, and Dad says, "Why should I pay ten bucks to see a house we should own?"

"Are you guys like super, super rich?" asks Sophie. Her eyes get wide when she asks this. She leans over, playing with her braids.

"My great-great-great-grandfather said he wanted his inventions to 'profit the world,' not his family."

"So you're not rich," says Sophie. "I didn't think so. Good thing you're not invited to my next party." She smiles when she says this, but it's not a joking smile. It's sort of a mean smile.

Sophie throws these huge birthday parties, but I think she enjoys not inviting kids to them more than she likes inviting kids to them.

She doesn't invite me every year.

But I don't care about her party. I care about finding those inventions. When I find them, I'll throw my own parties and I won't invite Sophie.

"Eddie, I think your great-great-great-grandfather was really sweet," says Chloe. "He wanted to profit the world. What a great man."

I shrug. "Profiting the world" makes no sense. If he left his money to us, maybe Mom and Dad wouldn't fight all the time about bills, and the bank wouldn't be trying to take our house.

At home, we have thin walls, so I hear things.

I've never been to the mansion, but I have something that will save my family.

I have a blueprint.

A blueprint is a house plan, and I have the original hand-drawn blueprint for the mansion. I found it crammed inside a pile of old newspapers sitting inside a big box of junk in our basement. Even my parents don't know I have this.

I take the blueprint out of my backpack. It only shows part of the house, but it has scribbles and notes written by my great-great-great-grandfather himself. I'm not sure what most of the notes mean.

But I know one thing for sure—if there is a hidden room, I will find it.

"What are you looking at?" asks Chloe.

I put down the blueprint. "Nothing."

"It looks like a map or something."

"It's nothing."

"It looks like something."

"It looks like you're being nosy."

Chloe turns her back to me to talk to Sophie. I feel sort of bad for snapping at her, but I am not sharing my blueprint with her, or anyone.

It's the map to my family's fortune, and to saving our home.

"I bet one of his secret inventions is a thermometer," says Kyle. He sits a few rows ahead, across from Brian and Seth. "But it predicts what your temperature will be tomorrow." Then he adds, in sort of a rap, "Take your temperature now—'cause here's the trick—you'll know today if tomorrow you'll be sick."

Kyle likes to rap a lot.

"If I invented a thermometer, it would always say I was sick. Then I'd just take my temperature every morning and never have to go to school," says Brian. Seth throws him a high five with a loud WHACK!

I groan and lift my blueprint again. No one knows what the inventions could be, but I hope they are way more incredible than a thermometer that says you're sick when you're not.

Those inventions, the treasures, are hiding in the mansion somewhere. They are just waiting for me to find them.

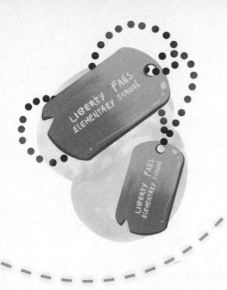

4

AARON

As the bus drives down the highway, Kyle jumps up. "No!" He looks really upset. His eyes are open extra wide. "She's gone!"

Jessie is on all fours looking on the floor in the aisle.

I'm about to ask what's going on when something twitters by my feet.

I bend down and scoop up a hamster. It looks like Soda, Mrs. Rosenbloom's class pet. I scratch Soda's head, between her little hamster ears. She purrs. She must like being scratched. "Look what I found," I say. I reach over to hand the hamster to Kyle.

"Get that rodent away from me!" Sophie shrieks, although the hamster isn't close to her. She curls into her seat and out of the aisle. "That almost touched me," she grumbles.

"Hamsters are cute and fuzzy," says Chloe.

"Hamsters are dumb," grunts Sophie.

"Everything okay back there?" asks Principal Klein from the front row.

"No problems at all!" Kyle shouts as he softly pets the hamster's fur. More quietly he adds, "I thought Soda would enjoy the trip. But I need to keep my backpack zipped."

As Kyle puts Soda into his backpack, I see straw sticking out and what looks like a small water bottle at the top. He's turned his backpack into a hamster home! He's even poked some holes in the top so she can breathe.

A few minutes later, the bus turns out of the main road and past an open black gate. The gate has huge swirly *M*s on both sides of it.

We drive down a long, winding driveway that zigzags through a bunch of trees and then comes out into a large green lawn the size of an army post. Way far away is the house. Even from back here I can see how ginormous it is.

It might be bigger than our school.

The mansion looks just as strange as it does in the pictures we saw in class. Maybe stranger. It reminds me of houses I made with LEGOs, adding rooms and walls until I ran out of pieces. The house is one floor tall in some places. Then it jumps up and stands seven floors high in others. Parts of the house look like they were stuffed into place, like no one knew where else to put them. Doors are where windows should be. There are eight chimneys, but only one of them is straight.

As we near the house, we pass mega-tall bushes. Each is trimmed into the shape of a food that Mr. Minks pickled. The row of Fantastic Food Foliage is sort of famous. One bush is shaped like a potato, one is shaped like a hot dog, and another is shaped like an ice-cream sundae. It took a long time to carve the nuts and whipped cream and the cherry on top.

"As I'm sure you know," says Principal Klein, turning around to face us, "Mr. Minks spent years trying to preserve food, mostly by pickling them. Pickling is keeping food in vinegar or salt to make it last longer. His pickled sardines fed hungry people in faraway countries. His pickled pig slop made hog farming easier and kept pigs healthier. He didn't always succeed but his motto was *Try, try again! And then try again! And then try a few more times after that, and then take a nap.*"

For such a great man, he didn't have such a great motto.

"Thomas Edison went through one thousand failed attempts at inventing the lightbulb before he succeeded," says Eddie. "The Legend of Liberty Falls only failed three times before he successfully pickled marshmallows."

"That's right," says Principal Klein.

"Mr. Minks could invent circles around Edison," says Eddie.

"He invented circles, too?" asks Brian.

Eddie rolls his eyes and mumbles to himself, "Why doesn't anyone make any sense?"

I see why no one talks to Eddie much.

Outside our bus, a tall and thin man in a long black coat trims one of the bushes—that bush is sort of shaped like a slice of pizza, I think. The man holds huge hedge clippers. He stares at our bus. I'm not scared of too many things, but eyeing this guy sends a shiver right through me.

SNNNIP!

A branch tumbles off the pizza bush.

I'm glad the bus keeps going. Dad says in the army you should always trust your instincts. He says that in the army, trusting your instincts can keep you alive.

And my instincts tell me not to trust the guy with the hedge clippers.

5
JESSIE

We pull up in front of the mansion. The driveway curves in a circle, around a tall marble statue of the famous Mr. Minks.

The inventor smiles and holds both his arms out, as if welcoming the world to his home. We learned that the statue used to be in the town square. When Mr. Minks first founded our town, he had a hard time getting people to move here, and he thought a friendly statue would help.

It must have worked, because our town is pretty big now.

The yard in front of the house and around the statue is all torn up. High mounds of dirt are piled next to deep holes. It's as if people were digging and digging and digging for something.

I wonder what they were looking for. I wonder if they found it.

The bus door opens, and we file out of the bus and onto the circular driveway.

A man in a tweed jacket walks out of the large double doors of the mansion, waving to us. His head is bald except for small tufts of curly gray hair over his ears.

"Welcome to the Minks Mystery Mansion," he says. "I am Claire St. Clare, the caretaker of this house. I am delighted you are here, although I must admit to some bad news—my assistant, Mrs. Vanderbilt, is home stuck in the flue."

"You mean stuck home *with* the flu," Mrs. Rosenbloom says.

Mr. St. Clare shakes his head. "No, I mean stuck *in* the flue. She was cleaning her chimney and got wedged in. I believe the fire department is at her home now." He sighs. "Anyway, Mrs. Welp, a volunteer from Liberty Falls Library, will lead half the tour today."

He points to a short woman in a bright purple jacket across the lawn. She stands by a bush carved into the shape of a doughnut. "Yoo-hoo, children!" She waves at us with a big, happy grin.

"This is Mrs. Welp's first trip to the house," says Mr. St. Clare. To Mrs. Welp he shouts, "Please join us, but be careful of the holes!"

Mrs. Welp, waving and smiling, takes three giant strides toward us and then disappears into the ground. "I'm quite all right." Her head pops up. "No worries. That's not the first hole I've walked into, and I'm sure it won't be the last." She climbs out of the hole, takes two steps forward, and then disappears into the ground. "Told you!"

Mr. St. Clare sighs. "We have most of our staff missing today, and I'm sure we'll be missing them terribly. We also have a whole lot of holes."

A cold wind that would freeze even my cats blows by us. I have a bad feeling about this trip. There's a creepy man with the hedge clippers, there are dark skies above us, and I heard a kid got lost in the mansion last year and they never found him.

I don't know if that's true, but I wish my cats were here. Cats can sense when things are wrong, which is why Fen, my Persian cat, sometimes doesn't come downstairs when Mama makes tofu nuggets for dinner. Mama says they taste like chicken, but she's not fooling me or Fen.

I think Fen would sense something is wrong here, too.

MiNKS MysterY
HANSION BluePRINT

6

EDDIE

"I hope you are all excited to learn about Mr. Minks and his inventions," says Mr. St. Clare. A few kids clap, but not me.

I'm not here to learn. I'm here to help my family get the secrets we were promised.

"Mr. Minks always said he wanted to create inventions that turned the world upside down," continues Mr. St. Clare. "In fact, he invented the upside-down cake. He didn't like people to desert the dinner table until after dessert."

"But if he turned the world upside down, wouldn't we all fall off?" asks Seth.

"Not if he invented gravity boots," says Brian. He and Seth high-five each other: SMACK!

"He didn't want to actually turn the world upside down," says Mr. St. Clare. "It means he hoped to make us see things differently."

"Is that why he built a room filled with inventions that no one knows about?" asks Brian.

"Can we look for it?" asks Seth. "I want an A-plus on my essay."

I grumble and shake my head. I can't have kids thinking about inventions or looking for inventions. Those inventions are the legacy my great-great-great-grandfather promised my family!

A legacy is what someone leaves you when they die. A legacy can be almost anything, like knowledge, or fame, or money. But if you ask me, a fortune is the best legacy of them all, especially when your dad is out of work.

"I'm afraid there are no secret inventions or a hidden secret invention room. The Mysterious Machines of Mr. Minks are nothing but myth. If inventions were hidden, their location would have been guessed by our guests long ago."

"You sure enjoy homonyms," says Principal Klein.

Mr. St. Clare blinks. "What's a homonym?"

"Never mind," says Principal Klein.

"If there were secret inventions, I bet one of them is an egg," says Seth. "But it's an egg that you eat, shell and all, and it hatches in your stomach so when you eat the egg it's like eating an entire chicken."

"That's gross," Sophie says.

"There are no inventions!" I growl, stomping my foot.

"Everyone quiet down, please," says Principal Klein. "Let's show Mr. St. Clare that the fifth graders of Liberty Fall Elementary are respectful. Now, before we begin our tour, I need everyone to choose a trip buddy. This is a large house, so stay with your trip buddy at all times."

Whenever we pick partners in class, I'm always stuck with the teacher. No one ever wants to be partners with me. Then I hear:

"Hey, um, want to be trip buddies?"

Aaron stands next to me. At first I assume he's talking to someone else, someone behind me. But there is no one behind me. I look at him. "Really?"

"Sure."

I chew my lip. A trip buddy can ruin everything. Sure, teaming with Aaron would be a lot better than being with a teacher. But I need to find inventions. A trip buddy—any trip buddy at all—will just be in the way.

Still, I'm so surprised to be asked, I gurgle out, "Um, okay."

I immediately regret saying that. Aaron smiles at me, but I need to set the ground rules now. I need to keep my distance.

"I don't really need a trip buddy," I add. "I mean, I won't get lost in this house. Not me. We can be trip buddies, but we're not going to be friends or anything."

"Um, okay," says Aaron, frowning back at me.

I take a deep breath. It would be great to make a new friend. Or to even have a friend. But not now. Not today.

Today isn't about making friends. It's about my family's legacy. It's about finding the fortune and keeping our house.

7
AARON

As I watch Norm pair up with Wesley, and Brian partner with Seth, I hear Sophie snap, "We both already have a partner, so go away."

She's talking to Anna. Strapped around Anna's shoulders is a mega-sized backpack. It's the biggest backpack I've ever seen. She could fit twenty books in there, easy. Why would she ever need to carry so many books?

Sophie glares at her.

"Never mind. I'll be my own buddy," mumbles Anna. She speaks so softly I can barely hear her. She looks down at her feet.

"You can join us. We can be a group of three," says Chloe with a cheerful smile.

"Are you kidding?" Sophie growls.

"Is there a problem?" asks Principal Klein, looking over.

"No problem!" shouts Sophie with a smile. Then she turns back to Anna and grumbles, "Fine. Whatever. As long as you don't stand near me. Or talk to me. Or breathe in my direction. And you're not invited to my next party, no matter what."

"Does anyone still need a partner?" asks Principal Klein. The group quiets down.

"Terrific," says Mr. St. Clare. "Then please say hello to Mr. Felix."

The tall and totally creepy guy we saw earlier, wearing the black coat and trimming bushes, walks through our group. "Excuse me, excuse me," he croaks. He still holds his large hedge clippers. I stare at them.

The guy makes me nervous.

Mr. St. Clare says, "Mr. Felix has been the groundskeeper at the Minks Mystery Mansion since he was a kid. I kid you not! Just like his father and grandfather."

Mr. Felix bows and smiles, but it's lopsided and he's missing a bunch of teeth. His smile makes me shudder.

"You must know so much about this house," Principal Klein says. "Do you have any words of wisdom for our students?"

"Do not touch things," says Mr. Felix in a hoarse rasp. "Do not snoop. Do not ask too many questions." He glares at us and then he loudly snips his hedge clippers.

SNIP!

I don't think I'll be touching, snooping, or asking many things—at least not around Mr. Felix.

"Mr. Felix is extremely busy, so he won't be joining us on our tour," says Mr. St. Clare. I take a big sigh of relief. "Half of you will join me, and half of your, uh, company will accompany Mrs. Welp."

Mrs. Welp, who has been standing in the middle of the lawn this entire time, beams with a giant grin. She takes three steps and then disappears. "I'm fine!" she shouts, her head poking out from another hole.

As she wiggles out from the ground, Principal Klein says, "Those of you in Mrs. Greeley's class will come with me and Mr. St. Clare. Mrs. Rosenbloom and her students can join Mrs. Welp."

Mrs. Rosenbloom mutters something under her breath. She doesn't look happy about going with Mrs. Welp, who has smudges of dirt on her face.

Mrs. Welp joins Mr. St. Clare on the sidewalk without falling into any more holes, and then she points left. "My group will begin at the milking barn and the horse stables."

"The stables are the opposite way," says Mr. St. Clare. Mrs. Welp wheels around. As she does, she stumbles. "Are you stable?"

"Oh yes. Perfectly fine, thank you." Mrs. Welp's face flushes. "Falling in holes just made me a little wobbly. I'm all straightened out now. This way!" She struts forward down the sidewalk, followed by Mrs. Rosenbloom and half the students.

"Do you think it's a good idea?" Mr. St. Clare calls after them. "Maybe we should skip the barn tour today? The storm looks awfully close." A few snowflakes fall.

"Nonsense. We'll be back in a jiffy," promises Mrs. Welp.

Their group follows a long winding path that leads to the back of the house.

"Our group will begin our tour *inside* the house," says Mr. St. Clare. "We'll visit the stables later, as long as the storm passes us by. But for now, please head to the front door."

As we walk toward the house, I hear the SNIP! SNIP! of hedge clippers behind me. Mr. Felix lingers on the sidewalk, watching us.

I walk toward the mansion just a little faster, away from those hedge clippers and the teeth-missing grin of the man snipping them.

8
JESSIE

"As you enter the house, please be careful not to touch anything," says Mr. St. Clare. He lingers behind us on the sidewalk next to Mr. Felix, who hasn't left yet. "And please stay together."

"You can count on our fifth graders," Principal Klein calls back. "They are the best-behaved kids you'll ever meet."

Next to me, Wesley says to Norm, "I'm touching everything." Norm nods in agreement.

Brian and Seth stand on the other side of me. Brian whispers to Seth, "First chance we get, let's sneak off and find that secret invention room."

Does Principal Klein really think we're the best-behaved kids you could ever meet? He should know better than that.

I walk at the end of the group. Vivian and I were going to pair up. Since she's sick, I don't have a trip buddy. But I don't need one. Cats are independent. And I can be, too.

Mama says it's good to be independent, which is why she makes me put away my dishes after dinner and sort my own laundry.

Behind me, Mr. Felix and Mr. St. Clare talk quietly. Mr. Felix makes me nervous. I may want to be independent like a cat, but I'm not brave like one.

Even when whispering, Mr. Felix's voice sounds scratchy and creepy. "I have begun." Snow falls around us. At first there are only a few flakes, but almost immediately they start dropping faster. "This storm can ruin everything."

"You're sure the inventions are safe?" asks Mr. St. Clare. "Even the ones that were in the safe?"

"Of course. Everything is on schedule." Mr. Felix rubs his hands together. "Then the money will roll in!"

"Sshh! Not so loud," says Mr. St. Clare. "I hate to talk about it."

"We're doing what needs to be done."

"I know. But I wish nothing needed to be done at all. Just be careful. The inventions are priceless." Mr. St. Clare's voice trembles a little. "They must not be damaged."

"Do you take me for a fool?" snaps Mr. Felix. "But even priceless inventions are worthless unless someone pays a price for them. And they will pay well."

I pause to listen closer. My cat Fen can sense when things are wrong, and my Fen-like cat senses are tingling.

"And the secret inventions? Have you found them?" asks Mr. St. Clare.

"Hopefully soon."

Mr. Felix stops speaking and glares when he sees me listening. All the other kids have already entered the house. Mr. Felix still holds those hedge clippers. He snips them. I gulp and speed up to join the rest of my class.

As I enter the house, his words and those of Mr. St. Clare float inside my head. Suddenly, I realize: They're going to steal the inventions. They're crooks! And they hope to find and swipe the secret inventions and steal them, too.

Someone needs to stop them!

I should stop them.

I would, if I were a cat.

Lucky for them, I'm just me, and what can I do?

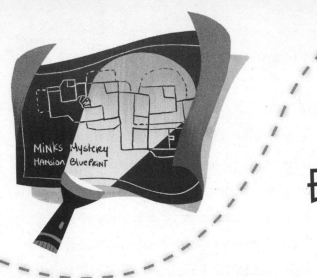

MINKs Mystery
MANSioN BluePRiNT

9

EDDIE

We walk through the door of the mansion and into a massive entryway. I bet a hundred people could fit in here. The entryway at my house only fits two people at one time, and it only fits one person if I don't put our shoes away.

The ceiling is two stories high. It appears to be made of solid gold. Hanging straight down is the world's largest ceiling fan. My great-great-great-grandfather invented ceiling fans.

And to think—all this should be my family's and mine.

Our legacy.

After I find those hidden inventions, my family will build a new house. My parents won't have to argue about money anymore. Instead, they'll argue about how big our ceiling fan will be.

Next to me is a coatrack. It's as large as a tree, with dozens of long wooden arms. I unzip my winter coat. The closest coatrack arm grabs my coat from me and then snaps back into place.

TWANG!

I jump back.

"Be careful! May I remind you not to touch anything," scolds Mr. St. Clare. "Just be thankful you're not wearing a hat." He pats the top of his mostly bald head, which has a long scratch on the top. "Mr. Minks only sold a few of his Sensational Spring-Coiled Coatracks and then spent years settling lawsuits over torn suits. He also invented the Sensational Spring-Coiled Shoe Rack, the Sensational Spring-Coiled Sock Rack, and the Sensational Spring-Coiled Underwear Rack. The less said about those inventions, the better."

I carefully step away from the coatrack and then look around the rest of the entryway. This room alone is worth more than my entire house. A grand staircase with golden handrails wraps itself around the room and up to the second floor. The floor is made of marble imported all the way from the North Pole.

Marble isn't even found in the North Pole, so my great-great-great-grandfather shipped marble to the North Pole, just so he could ship it back to the house.

He had so much money he didn't know what to do with it.

I don't know what I would do with that much money, but I certainly wouldn't spend it on shipping things back and forth to the North Pole.

I just need to find those secret inventions.

"This room is awesome," says Seth.

"Double awesome," says Brian, standing next to him.

"Wait. Aren't you both in Mrs. Rosenbloom's class?" Principal Klein asks. Brian and Seth nod. "Your class left with Mrs. Welp."

"I was wondering where everyone went," says Seth, scratching his head. "Brian and I were talking about the secret inventions and weren't paying attention."

"I thought one of the inventions might be a kite that's so long it reaches the moon," says Brian.

"But I said it would probably get tangled up in stars or maybe a rocket ship," says Seth. "What do you think?"

"I lost many kites in trees as a child," Principal Klein says, nodding. "So a kite that long could be a problem. You make a good point."

What? That's not a good point at all. That's just another invention idea that makes no sense.

"But your teacher might be worried about you," Principal Klein continues. He takes out a cell phone. "I better let her know you're with our group."

While he uses his phone, I turn my attention to the walls. They are covered in framed food photos. Next to me are photos of a banana, a plate of lasagna, a bowl of meatballs, and a pickle.

"Admiring the inventor's pickling portraits, I see," says Mr. St. Clare. "Just like the row of Fantastic Food Foliage outside, these are in honor of his proudest pickling achievements. Well, not the meatballs. You wouldn't want to eat the pickled meatballs." He shudders.

I point to the picture of a pickle. "He pickled a pickle?"

"No, that's the world's very first selfie. He invented the selfie."

"Um, that's not a selfie."

"Sure it is. Minks is wearing a pickle costume for a costume party." I squint, but it still just looks like a pickle to me. It must be a really good costume.

"Everyone to the grand ballroom," announces Mr. St. Clare.

We walk under the staircase and enter a room that must be the size of a soccer field. It's mostly empty except for several statues of my great-great-great-grandfather scattered about. The statues were sculpted by Rodin, a famous sculptor, and are worth a fortune.

"Mr. Minks built this marvelous grand ballroom to hold grand parties," says Mr. St. Clare.

"Did he throw parties often?" asks Principal Klein.

"No, never," says Mr. St. Clare, frowning. "Mr. Minks often discussed the disgust he had for parties. He was afraid people might break things."

"Mr. Minks wouldn't need to worry about anyone

breaking things with the fifth graders of Liberty Falls Elementary here," Principal Klein says.

"You can count on us," says Sophie, smiling at him.

Principal Klein beams at Sophie.

I shake my head.

"We'll all be extra careful," says Brian. He leans against one of the Minks statues. The statue wobbles, spins, falls over, and crashes to the ground. It breaks into a few hundred pieces. "Whoops."

There are a series of gasps and yelps from our class.

"We are so very sorry," Principal Klein says, his facing turning red.

Mr. St. Clare removes a tissue from his pocket and dabs sweat from his forehead. "No worries, no worries," he mumbles. "Fortunately, these statues are only replicas and not the originals."

"Where are the originals?" I ask.

Mr. St. Clare looks down at his shoes. He coughs, and then coughs again. His face reddens slightly, and he dabs his face again with his tissue. "Did you know that Mr. Minks invented flour made from flowers?" I shake my head. "Yes, most people thought the idea half-baked."

"That's great, but I was asking about the statues—"

Mr. St. Clare cuts me off. "If we have no other questions, we will now head to the inventor's private workshop."

That was strange. It was almost as if Mr. St. Clare avoided answering my question on purpose.

I can't worry about that. I need to keep my mind on what matters—finding the secret inventions and saving my family's house. If I were going to keep secret inventions, I'd probably keep them in my workshop or at least close by it. I bet there is a giant pile of the inventions in the corner of the room, and people have never found them because they have no sense.

Mr. St. Clare leads us through a side door and down a series of steps that ends at a giant drawing of a brain.

"Mr. Minks's invention room is right behind this picture," says Mr. St. Clare. "Children, this is where the magic happened. Prepare to be stunned. Electrified! Which reminds me, don't touch any of the outlets or you could be literally electrified. We've had some wiring problems. Anyway, I bring you—the inventor's workshop."

He pushes on the picture and it swings open. We all enter a huge room that's, to be honest, not so stunning or electrifying. In fact, it's almost completely empty. It's big—the room is probably bigger than my entire house—but the only things I see are an enormous sign hanging from the ceiling and, in the far corner, a small bed and a workbench.

If this room hides secret inventions, it hides them well.

"Why is the room so empty?" Principal Klein asks. "I thought this was his invention workshop."

Mr. St. Clare's face turns red. He still holds his tissue, and he wipes his brow. "Did you know that Mr. Minks invented mussels with muscles?" he asks. "He thought they had a stronger flavor that way."

"Sounds delicious," Principal Klein says.

"Well, if no one has any more questions, please look around," says Mr. St. Clare.

I look at Mr. St. Clare. I'm positive he purposely avoided answering that question about missing inventions, just like he avoided answering my question about the missing statues.

And Jessie keeps glaring at Mr. St. Clare with an evil eye.

Something is going on.

But I can't think about it. The sign hanging from the ceiling is much more interesting. It's so big it touches the floor. I can read it from here, even though the sign hangs on the other side of the room and I need new glasses.

START WORK AT 1

AND YOU WON'T HAVE ANY FUN.

BUT START WORK AT 01

AND YOU'LL HAVE A TON!

"What does that sign mean?" Aaron asks, pointing to the words I'm reading.

"No one knows," says Mr. St. Clare. "The inventor wrote poetry, but he wasn't good at it. He was not well versed in verses, versus inventing things. Still, this poem was his biggest."

"You mean his most famous?" Chloe asks.

"No," says Mr. St. Clare. "I mean it's his biggest, in terms of height. The sign stands twelve feet tall. He was very proud of it. Poets like to use big words."

I continue to stare at the huge poem. Mr. St. Clare is right about one thing—no one has ever figured out what that poem means. But it has to mean something, otherwise why did my great-great-great-grandfather make it so big?

Maybe it's a clue to the hidden invention room or a riddle that unlocks a secret message.

Or maybe my great-great-great-grandfather was just a bad poet and a weirdo.

Not a weirdo. Eccentric.

It doesn't matter what he was. What's important is that he left a legacy of secrets behind, and I intend to discover them first chance I get.

Meanwhile, Jessie keeps glaring at Mr. St. Clare, but I have no idea why.

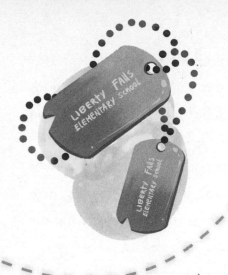

10

AARON

We're in the inventor's workshop, but it's sort of disappointing. I was expecting more stuff. Mr. St. Clare leads us to the corner of the room, which has a small bed and a workbench. We stand in a circle around them.

"Mr. Minks often worked nonstop," says Mr. St. Clare. "Why, he would work here for a week straight until he got so weak he needed a nap." He lifts a small shoe box that rests on the bench. "See this? It's one of Minks's greatest inventions."

"He invented the shoe box?" Brian asks.

"Of course not," says Mr. St. Clare with a chuckle. "This is Minks Entirely Edible Cardboard. You could make the food inside for dinner and then eat the box for dessert."

"Did people like it?" asks Seth.

"It depends on whether they enjoy cardboard that tastes like gym socks," says Mr. St. Clare. "It's good for stomach-aches—that is, if you can stomach the taste."

Mr. St. Clare picks up a small tube from the desk. "But this is even more incredible. My friends, this is Minks Amazing Almost Forever Paste." Mr. St. Clare flicks the lid off the tube with a soft PLIP! "Mr. Minks paced for hours while coming up with the formula for this paste. This amazing glue bonds two things together instantly and almost forever."

He pops the lid back on and places the tube on the bench. He lifts his hand up and the Almost Forever Paste tube lifts, too. It looks like the tube is stuck to him. Mr. St. Clare shakes his hand, but the tube doesn't move. He tries to pull the tube off, but it won't budge. Even worse, both of his hands are now stuck together. "Um, one moment, please," he says. His face turns red as he tries to tear his hands apart.

"Let me help," says Principal Klein. He reaches for the tube with both hands. He gives it a tug.

And now it seems Principal Klein's hands are stuck, too.

The two men grunt and pull and pant and heave. They stumble this way and that way, but their hands are glued together.

"I've got it! I've got it!" Principal Klein shouts between grunts. "Um, no I don't."

Principal Klein and Mr. St. Clare pull and wheeze. That Amazing Almost Forever Paste is strong. We learned that builders use it to bond skyscrapers together.

"Are you going to be like that forever?" asks Jessie.

"Fortunately, this is Almost Forever Paste," says Mr. St. Clare, panting. "It sticks forever unless you use Never Forever Spray. We always keep a bottle on the workbench." He looks at Jessie, who stands near him. "Would you spray some on us, miss? Just don't miss."

Jessie lifts a small bottle from the workbench. She squirts the clear and watery spray on Mr. St. Clare's and Principal Klein's hands. With a POP! both men's hands come loose, and the tube falls to the floor.

Principal Klein must have still been yanking backward to free his hands, because he spins and falls on the floor with a loud THWUMP!

"Oh no. Are you okay?" asks Mr. St. Clare.

"Quite all right," Principal Klein says with a groan. He gets up from the floor and rubs dust from the seat of his pants and his orange cardigan sweater.

"Sticking together was a sticky situation," says Mr. St. Clare. "But this is still my favorite room in the entire mansion." He closes his eyes. "Sometimes I stand in this room and imagine myself inventing something. And sometimes I stand here glued to the workbench until someone finds me." He opens his eyes, clears his throat, and smiles. "We should go to the next room. We have so much to see and so little time to see it."

We follow him back across the room. As we walk, Eddie scans the floor. He bends down and rubs his finger across it.

"What are you doing?" I ask.

Eddie jumps up, surprised, his mouth open. "I'm, um, admiring the floor. This floor is very nice."

"It's just a floor."

"Then you don't know anything about floors," he says. He clears his throat and lifts his chin. His surprised, open mouth has been replaced with a smug frown. "Which shows how little you know about anything."

Figures. I picked the one trip buddy who doesn't want a buddy.

I watch Eddie walk away. I don't know if I can figure him out. It's like he is going out of his way to be as unlikeable as possible.

And for someone who says he comes to this house every week, he certainly doesn't act like it. He looks around the rooms as much as everyone else, maybe even more. He keeps staring at things and watching things.

I have a feeling there are a few things Eddie isn't telling me.

11

JESSIE

Mr. St. Clare—the thief!—leads us out of the inventor's workshop and back to the grand ballroom. We then head to the entryway and up the large golden staircase.

"This part of the house was built ten years after the main part was built," says Mr. St. Clare. "They had to hire lots of people to build the house higher."

There are a series of paintings in the hallway, each the size of a door.

The first one we see is a painting of a pickle.

"Minks is most famous for his pickling, of course. Well, behind this painting is the inventor's pickling room, where he did most of his experiments. I hope you all like pickles."

Mr. St. Clare smiles and pushes the portrait, which swings open to reveal the room behind it. We all file inside.

Shelves line the walls, each filled with jars of pickles.

Giant bottles of salt and vinegar are on top of the table, and sitting on the ground are giant oak barrels.

But the thing I notice most is the smell. The room smells like fish—very old and sour fish. I immediately want to take a shower. I have to plug my nose to keep the stink out.

"What is that odor?" asks Principal Klein, his eyes watering.

"The inventor spent many years perfecting his pickling techniques," says Mr. St. Clare with a sigh. "Unfortunately, they produced a strong, fishlike scent. Some say it smelt like smelts. We've bleached the room, scrubbed the room, and even lined it with rows of roses. But the smell remains. You get used to it after a while."

"A long while, I imagine," says Principal Klein, gagging.

"Did you know the inventor first named this town Pickled Falls?" asks Mr. St. Clare. "He had a hard time getting anyone to move here, though. Lady Minks suggested they rename it Liberty Falls, and the rest is history."

"Can we go to another room, please?" Principal Klein asks, his face turning blue from holding his breath.

Mr. St. Clare's shoulders sag. "Are you sure? I haven't shown the students how to properly pickle moldy cheese." He points to the table. "It's always a tour highlight, although I should warn you it can get a bit smelly. They don't smell as bad as pickled meatballs, though." He shudders.

"No, really, I think we'll pass on the experiments," says our principal, tears streaming down his cheeks, his face turning bluer.

"It's no problem. We keep a barrel of pickle juice downstairs, along with a barrel of one-hundred-and-fifty-year-old pickles," says Mr. St. Clare. I don't think he's noticed our principal's face has gone from blue to purple. "No?" Our principal's face is bright violet. Mr. St. Clare sighs. "Very well, then. On to the next room."

Our entire class rushes toward the door. "No pushing," Principal Klein says, but he's in just as much of a hurry to escape this room as the rest of us.

He rushes past me and I wonder if I should tell him what I heard. Should I warn him about Mr. St. Clare and Mr. Felix and how they are going to steal everything in the house? We need to alert the police! The FBI!

No. He would never believe me.

I wouldn't believe me.

And right now I just need to get out of this room and away from that horrible stench.

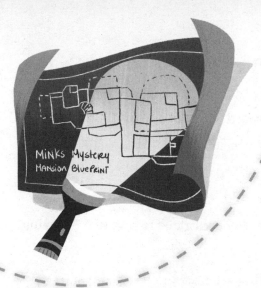

MiNKS Mystery Mansion Blueprint

12
EDDIE

We visit a guest bedroom, a playroom, a few bathrooms, and some other places, but nothing that would hide a secret invention. I'm getting restless. Then Mr. St. Clare leads our group to a large painting of a candle.

"We will now enter the inventor's study, which is where the inventor studied," says Mr. St. Clare. He pushes open the painting, and we walk inside. Standing inside is Mr. Felix.

Just looking at him makes me feel nervous.

Mr. Felix holds a large sack over his shoulder. He slumps a bit. The bag must be heavy.

"Mr. Felix!" says Mr. St. Clare. "Hi. I didn't expect to find you this high."

"Just gathering things," says Mr. Felix.

"Don't let us keep you. I know you have much to do."

Jessie glares at Mr. Felix, and then at Mr. St. Clare, and

then glares again at Mr. Felix. She shakes her head. She even growls, I think.

Mr. Felix lumbers toward the door, grunting from the weight of that bag. What's inside? He brushes past me, and part of his arm touches my hand.

I shiver. His arm is ice-cold.

Jessie watches him leave, her eyes glued to him like Amazing Almost Forever Paste.

But I need to stop paying attention to Jessie and start paying attention to this room.

It's a serious room, with dark wood panels, a large wooden desk, and a big brown leather chair. Mr. Minks must have done some serious studying here.

Did he hide serious secrets here, too?

A bookcase stands against the wall. It's almost completely empty, with only a couple of magazines sitting on it. I wonder if it used to be full. If it was, where did the books go?

"As you know, Mr. Minks was the world's greatest inventor," says Mr. St. Clare. "Or maybe the world's second-greatest inventor. Top three for sure." While everyone stands around the desk and listens to Mr. St. Clare talk about Minks and how the town came to be, I slink to the empty bookshelf. There's a door next to it. Maybe while everyone's preoccupied,

I can slip away and explore. No one will notice if I'm gone. No one ever notices me.

I look back at the group and turn the knob. I step out, still checking to make sure no one is watching.

A gust of wind smashes into me, but something yanks me back by my belt.

The door stays open and swings against the side of the house with a THUNK! Cold air and snow blow into the house as I fall back. The magazines on the bookshelf flutter from the wind gusts.

I came about an inch from falling out of the house and landing in the front yard.

As I stare out the open door, I'm surprised how much snow is outside. The yard is almost completely covered already, and it's still coming down in blankets. It looks like a snow globe out there.

It's then that I notice Aaron is behind me. He is the one who grabbed my belt. He saved my life!

Before I can say anything, Mr. St. Clare pulls a rope hanging next to the bookshelf and the door slams shut.

Principal Klein wags his finger at me. "What were you doing, Eddie? You've been told not to touch things. Someone could have gotten hurt."

"I don't know, sir. It's just that, um, I adore doors."

Mr. St. Clare sniffs, but the answer seems to calm him a little.

"Our students are normally very responsible," Principal Klein says to Mr. St. Clare. "I don't know what has gotten into them today. I promise no one will touch anything else." He glares at our class. It's a warning glare.

He doesn't have to say anything else for us to get the message.

Mr. St. Clare sniffs. "I suppose there's been no damage done. But perhaps we should go somewhere without dangerous doors. Please follow me to the next room."

As the class walks out, I turn to Aaron, who stands next to me. "Thanks."

"No problem. We're trip buddies."

"I know, but if you hadn't grabbed me . . ."

"You'd do the same for me, right?"

"Um, sure." I smile.

Would I have done the same for him? I don't know. I haven't been nice to Aaron. Maybe I should be nicer. I barely know him, but I could use some help finding those inventions.

Maybe Aaron can help me find my family's legacy.

No, a Minks never needs anyone. That's what my dad always says: "That no-good Minks left us nothing, but we don't need anything from anyone anyway."

It's up to me to save my family, and me alone.

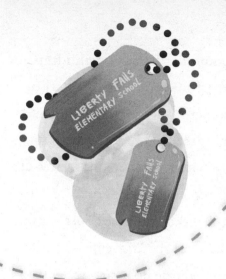

13

AARON

I'm glad I saw Eddie opening that door just in time, and for a second, he seemed thankful and friendly. He even smiled at me. But then his nose lifted and the same old Eddie was back.

He stomped away from me after that, but he can't get rid of me that easily. In the army, you support your fellow soldiers, no matter what. I know that Eddie and I aren't soldiers, but we're trip buddies. So I'm going to help him, whether he wants my help or not.

In the hallway, Mr. St. Clare leads us to another painting on a door. It's a painting of a skunk. We already survived a room that smelled like fish pickles. If this is a room of skunks, there is no way I'm going in.

"Guess what this room is," says Mr. St. Clare.

"Uh, a room of skunks?" Brian guesses.

"No, no, no," says Mr. St. Clare with a chuckle. "His struggle to perfect pickling wasn't the only pickle Mr. Minks found himself in. This is his room of failed invention ideas—ideas that didn't quite gel, like permanent hair gel. It turns your hair into cement. I put some on my own hair just last year." He sighs and pats the top of his bald head. "Turned out to be a bad idea. Still, this is an important room. Many of Minks Miserable Mistakes inspired later inventions."

"But why is there a painting of a skunk on the door?" I ask.

"Because Mr. Minks thought all of these inventions stunk, of course." Mr. St. Clare swings open the door, and we enter a room that's exactly half-empty. There are a whole bunch of strange things on the right side of the room, on shelves and on the ground.

But nothing at all is on the left side of the room.

It's like someone decided to remove exactly half of the things in the room.

"Why is the room only half-full?" asks Principal Klein.

Mr. St. Clare looks away, and his face flushes a bit. "So! Did you know Minks invented steak on a stake? Perfect for the grill, but today they're quite rare. Well, if you have no more questions, let's take a closer look at some of the miserable mistakes."

Jessie glares at Mr. St. Clare, and Eddie watches Jessie glaring.

With all this glaring from Jessie and sneaking from Eddie, I feel like a whole bunch of things are happening right under my nose.

As Mr. St. Clare shows us things, I tap on Eddie's shoulder. "Why did you open the door?"

Eddie looks back at me with a blank look on his face. A *what are you talking about* look. "What do you mean?"

"You come to this mansion all the time, right? That's what you said on the bus. So in the last room, you must have known that door led to thin air before you opened it. So why did you open it?"

Eddie looks away, and then looks back at me. "It's just . . ." He stops. He stares at me. It's as if he's thinking really hard about what to say next.

"Yes?"

"Nothing. Of course I knew about that door. I just wanted to see the snow outside." The *what are you talking about* look is now his normal *I'm way better than you* look. "I even have my own bedroom here."

Then Eddie turns and walks away from me.

I don't believe he has a bedroom here. Not for a minute. I don't believe he opened the door to look at the snow, either. He was about to fall out the door.

Why is he lying?

14
JESSIE

Mr. St. Clare points to a large blue tank sitting in the corner of the failed inventions room. Dozens of small pipes stick out of it, each capped with a bright red rubber tip. "You are looking at the Minks Breathtaking Balloon Machine, the world's fastest water balloon maker. One twist of the knob fills sixty-two water balloons and ties off the tips. The tying of the tips was a tip from Lady Minks. It works like a charm."

"Then why is it a failed invention?" Chloe asks.

"It was outlawed," says Mr. St. Clare. "If you got into a water balloon fight with the Minks Breathtaking Balloon Machine, you couldn't lose. The National Water Balloon Championship of 1882 ended in a ten-way tie when every finalist smuggled one in. It was quite the scandal."

"When I was a boy, I wanted to be a professional water-ballooner," says Principal Klein with a frown. "But I became a principal instead."

"And what's that?" Chloe asks. She points to a red, white, and blue fluffy backpack.

"That holds the Death-Defying Gravity Pack—the world's first parachute," says Mr. St. Clare. He dances over to the pack and lifts it. Dust sprinkles off. "After you jumped, you'd untie a tie, unknot a knot, unhook a hook, unfold twelve different folds, and poof! Out came the parachute."

"That seems like a lot to do while you're plummeting to earth," Principal Klein says.

Mr. St. Clare sighs and puts down the pack. "That's why it's a failed invention. Mr. Minks had his brother Alfred test it for him. I hear Alfred was two feet shorter after that jump."

I notice a small vacuum cleaner with a big pink sponge sticking out of the side. "Is that some sort of cleaning machine?"

"Exactly right. It's a Fantastically Fabulous Feline Groomer. Mr. Minks loved animals and thought cats might get tired of licking their fur all the time. This machine licked their fur for them! No one was interested in it, though."

I squeal with excitement. That sounds like the best invention ever. I would buy one for all my cats: Patches, Oscar, and Fen.

At least that's one great invention Mr. Felix and Mr. St. Clare haven't stolen. I've been watching Mr. St. Clare like a hawk. He hasn't done anything too suspicious. Not yet. But when he does, I'll be ready.

I'm not sure what I'll be ready to do, though.

If my cats were here, they'd know what to do. I bet my house cat Oscar could read his mind, and then he'd know everything about their evil plan. Mama says I'm as nutty as a box of weasels, but I'm sure Oscar can read people's minds. Sometimes when I think of Oscar at home, he'll wander into my room and jump on my bed.

Mr. St. Clare leads us back out into the hallway. We pass a full-length painting of a dark, winding, and gloomy staircase.

"What's behind there?" I ask.

"A dark, winding, and gloomy staircase," says Mr. St. Clare. "It's the fastest way upstairs."

"Are we going up?" Chloe asks.

"I'm afraid only the bottom two floors are open to the public today," says Mr. St. Clare.

"How come?" I ask.

Mr. St. Clare looks away. "Um, did you know that Mr. Minks invented a twelve-carat-gold carrot cake? It tasted like chocolate, but most people found it too rich. Anyway, if we have no more questions, let's continue."

Mr. St. Clare might have everyone else fooled, but he's not fooling me. I know why we're not touring the upper floors. I know why he keeps avoiding answering anytime we ask about empty rooms.

It's because he can't admit the truth! Mr. Felix is probably loading stolen inventions onto a truck somewhere right now!

If I had my cats here, I would stop him.

Our group stops in front of a painting that's twice as big as any other painting in the hallway. The picture has a hundred things painted on it. There are wheels and lightbulbs and rakes and windmills and baseball bats and boats and pelicans and balloons and bicycles and a telescope and a telegraph and a sewing machine and more.

"What's in *this* room?" I ask.

"Open the door and see," says Mr. St. Clare with a small smile.

I touch the painting. I'm nervous. What can be in a room that has so many things painted on its door?

But everyone is looking at me, so I take a deep breath, push open the painting, and step into the room.

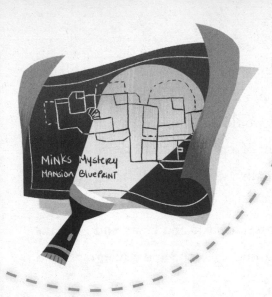

15

EDDIE

This entire tour has been a waste. Sure, we've seen some interesting things. But I don't care about interesting. I care about
fortune.

I scratch at a crack in the plaster wall, but it's just a
crack. I nudge a pickle picture, thinking maybe if there's
something behind it. There's nothing. I tap a candleholder
on the wall, wondering if it will move and a secret door will
slide over.

Nope.

Then Jessie opens a door with a million things painted on
it, and I follow our group into a new room. My eyes go wide as
we enter the famous Minks Mystery Mansion library. It's
massive. Bookshelves line the walls, floor to ceiling. Every
shelf is crammed full.

That explains the painting. This is a room where you can
find almost anything.

My great-great-great-grandfather wrote most of these books himself. I don't know how he found the time to write so many things and think of thousands of inventions and spend so much time studying pickles.

So many books! Any one of them could hold the secret to the secret room.

I rub my hands together, excited.

Because I know something about this room that no one else knows.

This room has a secret. Or at least I think it has a secret. I'm just not sure what the secret is.

On my blueprint my great-great-great-grandfather scribbled a note next to this very library. I don't even have to take out the blueprint to know what he jotted down:

BOOK your TRAVEL to the E-X-I-T.

It was written just like that! I wish I knew what it meant. It's a mystery, like so many other things about this place.

"There are exactly nine hundred books in this library," says Mr. St. Clare. "Nine hundred was Mr. Minks's favorite number. He even wrote a poem about it. *I wrote many books, exactly nine hundred. Everyone will love them, even the undead.*"

"The undead?" Seth asks.

"It's not a good poem," says Mr. St. Clare with a sigh. "Unfortunately, few words rhyme with *hundred.*"

"Bun thread," says Brian. "That rhymes."

"And sun bread," says Seth.

"Exactly my point." Mr. St. Clare shows the class more books. While everyone listens, I see my chance. I slink to the back and study the shelves for hints. There are books about engineering and farming. There are books about subjects we learn in school, like history and math. There are even two books about recess. An entire shelf is filled with road atlases from cities and countries around the world. There must be a dozen sets of encyclopedias.

But if any of these books hold the secret of how to find a hidden invention room, I can't tell from their covers. And there are too many books to search all of them.

I remove the blueprint from my back pocket.

My great-great-great-grandfather drew a box right where I'm standing. That must mean something. There's an arrow pointing to his mystery message:

BOOK your TRAVEL to the E-X-I-T.

"What's that?" Aaron looks over my shoulder. I didn't see my trip buddy walk up to me.

I lower the blueprint. "Nothing."

"That looks like a map or something," says Aaron.

"No it's not."

Aaron leans in closer, trying to peek at my blueprint. "Are you looking for something? Maybe I can help. I'm pretty good at finding stuff."

What if I tell him what I'm looking for, and he decides to steal all the inventions for himself?

I eye him and frown.

He smiles.

I gulp.

He saved my life. But can he help save my family?

I speak in a whisper. "You can't tell anyone about this. Our secret, okay?"

"Okay."

I check once again to make sure no one is paying attention to us. Of course they aren't. No one ever pays attention to me. They all listen to Mr. St. Clare.

I show Aaron the blueprint. I tell him what it is and where I found it.

"Wow." Aaron stares at it. "And it is the original?"

"I think so."

Aaron nods. "But why do you need it?"

I bite my lip, unsure how much I should tell Aaron and how much I can trust him. "Let's just say there might be some stuff that maybe no one has found. And maybe this blueprint shows them."

"What do you mean?"

I shrug.

"Like a secret invention room?"

I shrug again.

"You think you can find . . ."

He doesn't finish the sentence. I don't say anything, but Aaron isn't dumb.

That's why he can help me.

I point to the blueprint, showing him where we stand. "We're right here, in the middle of this box. Now look at this." I point to the message. "That has to be a clue, right? A clue to something."

"Book your travel to the exit," Aaron reads, nodding. "Some of those words are in all caps. And the word *exit* is written with dashes. That might mean something, too."

"I know. But what?"

"We must now head to the next room," says Mr. St. Clare. He waves his arms to lead our group back out to the hallway.

My chance is slipping away. As kids follow Mr. St. Clare out of the room, Aaron and I linger behind. Aaron stares at the blueprint and then at the bookshelves next to us. "These are road atlases." I nod. "Those are sort of like travel books, right?" He thumbs through the books. "Book your travel. Travel books."

"So maybe one of these travel books leads to a hidden room?" The atlases are from all over the world, big countries and small towns I've never heard of. My great-great-great-grandfather couldn't have hidden the secret invention room in another country. If he did, I'll never find it.

The last few kids stream out the door. Principal Klein might notice us missing at any moment.

Aaron still stares at the blueprint, thinking. "The way he spelled *exit* . . . ," he says. "E-X-I-T. What if he was spelling out the first letters of the travel books?" He removes the atlas for Egypt. "Egypt. That could be the *E*." Then he removes a travel book for the Xinjiang Province. "This has to be the *X*. There are no countries that begin with *X*." He removes the atlas for Iceland and then says, "Now we just need a *T*. Should I remove Turkey or Trinidad?"

"Both?"

Aaron slides both of those books from the shelf. As soon as he does, the floor opens up underneath us.

We fall through a trapdoor.

Everyone else has left the room, so I don't think anyone hears my scream.

16
CHLOE

This has been the most funtastic field trip ever. *Funtastic* is a word I made up myself. It means fun and fantastic!

Sophie has been in a bad mood most of the day, though. I feel bad. It's sort of my fault. She didn't want Anna to be our trip buddy, and I invited Anna anyway.

Sophie acts mean sometimes, but deep down she's nice. She just doesn't like to show people that side of her. We have these sleepovers and we spend the whole night giggling about funny things.

Although, now that I think of it, during our last few sleepovers she spent most of the night saying mean things about people. She's been meaner ever since she got a new baby brother. I think he's funtastic, but Sophie complains that her house smells like diapers all the time.

There are more rooms down the hall, and I bet each and

every one is super funtastic. But we don't walk down the hall. Instead, Mr. St. Clare waves us back over to the grand staircase. "The rest of this floor is off-limits today."

"Why is it off-limits?" Brian asks.

Mr. St. Clare coughs and dabs his head with a tissue. "Um, here's a fun fact. Mr. Minks invented a cough syrup for animals. His horse would often get hoarse, you see. Unfortunately, few would pony up any money to buy it. Well, if there are no more questions, let's head downstairs."

Mr. St. Clare knows so many interesting things!

But why does Jessie keep staring at him and shaking her head?

We stand at the top of the stairs, looking down. The view from up here is even better than funtastic. It's wondertastic!

"It's beautiful," says Principal Klein.

I look outside a window over the door, but I can't even see the sky through all the falling snow. The blizzard keeps getting worse and worse.

We walk down the stairs and gather at the bottom. At least I think it's all of us. Our group seems a little smaller than before, but I'm probably imagining it.

Principal Klein must notice the same thing, because he asks, "Are we all here? Is anyone missing their trip buddy?" When no one says anything, he smiles. "All right, then."

"Let's head down into the basement next," says Mr. St. Clare. "Basements were a luxury when this house was built. Sellers charged extra for building cellars."

"This whole tour is dumb," Sophie whispers into my ear.

I think it's fascinating. But I don't say anything. Sophie might just get mad. I'm usually careful not to make Sophie mad. That's what makes us such good friends.

Sophie Jarrell and Chloe Reynolds! The terrific twosome! That's us. That's been us for as long as I can remember. We even wear matching best friend necklaces.

At least I wear a best friend necklace.

"Where's your necklace?" I ask Sophie. I don't see one dangling around her neck.

"I'm not sure," she says. "It's somewhere, I think."

"That's okay," I say, and fake a smile to hide my frown. Maybe we're not a terrific twosome anymore?

Mr. St. Clare leads us to a small door near the coatrack. "Here we are. The light is broken, so please watch your step."

Mr. St. Clare leads the way down the stairs, and Principal Klein waits for us all to follow. "After you, after you," Principal Klein says.

We walk down a long flight of stairs. The steps creak beneath our feet. It's so dark, I can't see a thing.

I'm glad I'm with my entire class. I can't imagine walking down these unlit stairs alone. The staircase steps creak and creak. I find a handrail, but it feels like sandpaper and slightly sticky. So I don't use the handrail.

CREAAKKK. CREAAKKK.

Sophie steps on my heel, and my shoe flips off my foot. I stop to bend down to pick it up, but since it's dark, Sophie doesn't stop. She bumps into me, and I almost fall forward.

I grab the rough and sticky handrail.

"Be more careful," growls Sophie.

"I lost my shoe," I say. "I'm sorry that I made you bump into me."

Downstairs, a light turns on. Mr. St. Clare must have reached the bottom. It's still a long way down, but at least I can see my shoe! It rests on the next step. I slip my foot back into it.

My sock is happier with a shoe around it.

"Hurry up," hisses Sophie.

"Sorry again," I say.

"Why do you always say 'sorry' so much?"

"I don't know. Sorry about saying sorry. And sorry for saying sorry that time, also."

We reach the bottom.

"Welcome to the blue room," says Mr. St. Clare. "It looks very sunny here. Doesn't it, sonny?" he asks Brian.

"Sure," Brian answers.

We're in a big rec room that is completely yellow. The walls are the color of a lemon, and large mustard-yellow leather couches with big fluffy mustard-yellow pillows sit against the wall. The floor is covered with shaggy, bright banana-yellow carpet. There's even a pool table that's yellow, and all the balls on it are yellow, too.

Yellow is a happy color. I can't help but smile.

"Why are you grinning?" asks Sophie.

I stop smiling.

"Why is this called the blue room?" Principal Klein asks. "Everything in this room is yellow."

Mr. St. Clare nods. "Minks was color-blind. He thought everything here was blue, except for the blinds." He points to a small window with red blinds covering it. "He thought those were green."

"How about this?" asks Brian. He holds up a small orange rug that sat under the yellow pool table. "What color did he think this was?"

Mr. St. Clare points to the ground, his mouth open. "Step away!" he shouts to Brian.

Under the pool table is a small net. A rope runs from the net, along the ground, and then disappears into the carpet.

Mr. St. Clare walks toward it, slowly. "My boy, one foot closer and your foot may have been caught in that net, and a split second later you'd have been swinging from the ceiling. I'd be quite down if we had to cut you down."

"What is it?" Brian asks.

"A ghost trap," says Mr. St. Clare. "I thought we had uncovered them all, but it appears we missed one. Lady Minks set them up throughout the house."

"Did she ever catch a ghost?" asks Sophie. She shivers slightly when she asks.

"I don't think so. Lady Minks was terribly frightened of ghosts. She would have been in very bad spirits if she ever actually caught a spirit. Anyway, please step far away from the pool table—carefully now—and follow me." Mr. St. Clare points toward a large picture that's painted completely white. "I want to show you the green room."

"Being color-blind is dumb," says Sophie.

I just sigh.

Mr. St. Clare opens the door, and we go inside. A large clothesline stretches across the room. Dozens of white sheets hang from it. In the corner of the room is a large white metal box with a person-sized hamster wheel attached.

"Lady Minks wore up to twenty-two outfits every day, so Minks built the Minks Wonderful Workout Washer—the world's first automatic washing machine and exercise wheel," explains Mr. St. Clare. "The servants ran in the wheel, which powered the cleaning brushes. The clothes would be in great shape, and so would the servants."

Principal Klein points to the clothesline. "All those hanging sheets almost look like ghosts," he says, chuckling.

Sophie bites one of her nails.

Mr. St. Clare nods. "Ghosts. Yes. That's why Lady Minks never came down here."

Sophie bites another of her nails.

Just then, one of the baskets moves. The sheets in the basket spill out. One sheet floats in the air! Sophie gasps and grabs my arm so tightly it hurts. She yells, "The house is haunted!"

Principal Klein steps forward, as if he's going to protect us.

Sophie digs her fingers into my arm. It's super painful. But then the floating white sheet falls to the ground, and Aaron waves to us. Eddie sticks his head out of the basket.

Sophie lets go of my arm. There are still red marks on it from her grip. My arm does not feel funtastic.

"Sorry if we, um, scared you," says Aaron. "We sort of fell down the laundry chute."

"What were you doing messing with the laundry chute?" demands Principal Klein. "Was this your idea of some sort of prank?"

"No, sir, of course not, sir," says Aaron. "There was a trapdoor in the library and we fell down. It was an accident."

"There isn't a trapdoor in the library," says Mr. St. Clare. He shakes his head and wags his finger. "I know all the secret doors. So you could not shoot down a chute."

"That's what happened," says Aaron. "We moved some books, and the door opened up."

Mr. St. Clare stares at them. I don't think he believes them.

Meanwhile, Principal Klein does not think this is funtastic—not one bit. He shakes his head and folds his arms. He glares at Eddie and Aaron. "You were told not to touch things."

Aaron looks down at his shoes. "We made a mistake. Sorry, sir."

"You two are very lucky," Principal Klein says, shaking his finger. "You could have easily gotten hurt or lost. Try to be more like Sophie." He points to Sophie. She smiles but is still trembling. She is really scared of ghosts.

"I wouldn't get lost," says Eddie. "I have a—" Then he stops talking and bites his lip.

"What do you have?" asks Principal Klein.

Eddie's face turns red. He stammers. "Um . . ."

"An excellent sense of direction," says Aaron. "Eddie has an excellent sense of direction, so he wouldn't get lost." Aaron sort of looks away when he says this.

I think it's great that Eddie has such a good sense of direction. I wish I did.

"It's easy to get turned around in this house," says Mr. St. Clare. "If we are all here, we should head back upstairs." He looks out the window and checks his watch. "Look at the time! I'm sorry we didn't visit the barn, but with all this snow it was best to stay indoors. Still, I hope you have all learned something today."

I flash Sophie a big smile. "Wasn't this trip super great?"

Sophie frowns. "I thought it was dumb."

Principal Klein is right ahead of us and he's talking on his cell phone. He puts it down and shakes his head. "I have some bad news. We're not going anywhere. We're snowed in."

17
AARON

We walk up the stairs and into the grand ballroom. Mr. St. Clare and Principal Klein huddle together, talking. Principal Klein has a loud voice, but I can hear both of them.

"The buses are trying to get through," says Principal Klein. "Still, it could be hours."

"Oh my, oh my," says Mr. St. Clare.

"Can we stay here? Is that a problem?"

Mr. St. Clare bites his lip. Then he sighs. "Of course not." He doesn't sound too happy about it, though.

"But I wonder where Mrs. Rosenbloom and her students are. I spoke to her a couple of hours ago. They were still at the barn and were about to head back."

"Then they must be here, even if we don't hear them," says Mr. St. Clare. "It's a big house."

"Yes, that must be it. They'll be joining us any minute now. I'll text her and ask."

I gulp. I hope everyone is in the house. What if Mrs. Welp's group never came back? I think of them outside, in this ginormous blizzard.

"The kids will be hungry," says Principal Klein. "Do you have any food? Something they could eat for dinner?"

Mr. St. Clare scratches his head. "We don't keep much food in the house." He scrunches his lips. "Let me think. We have the bucket of one-hundred-and-fifty-year-old pickles. The children may enjoy an authentic antique Minks pickle."

Principal Klein shivers. "I doubt they would enjoy that."

"Perhaps. Kids are picky. I know! We also have a stack of boxes made from Entirely Edible Cardboard in the kitchen."

Principal Klein frowns. "Um, anything else?"

"I keep an emergency box of granola bars in the front closet."

"That sounds perfect."

"I'm afraid there won't be enough for everyone, and I don't want kids fighting over granola bars."

"That would be a problem," Principal Klein agrees.

No one else is paying attention to them, but I notice Sophie listening intently to the conversation. She has a small smile on her lips. I'm not sure why.

"Now that I think of it, Mr. Felix keeps a tub of oatmeal in the kitchen," says Mr. St. Clare. "I'll have him prepare a bowl for each student. Please escort the children to the dining room.

We have ketchup and grape juice you can pass out, too. We may even have a loaf of bread. It will be a feast!"

Principal Klein leads us to the dining room, which is just past the grand ballroom. As we walk, I peek out the window. It's like the entire world turned white.

"What's that?" asks Brian. A large wooden contraption sits in the corner of the room, tied together with ropes, sort of like a large slingshot.

"That is the inventor's famous meal catapult," says Mr. St. Clare. "Put a plate on the catapult, and a meal would fly right to you. It saved lots of time setting the table, but made dinnertime quite messy."

Principal Klein sighs. "I built one myself when I was a kid. We never did get the spaghetti sauce stains off the ceiling."

Our class fits on one long wooden table. I spot Eddie at the end, alone. I grab the seat next to him. "Do you think Mrs. Rosenbloom's class is okay?"

Eddie nods. "Of course. What could have happened to them?"

"Nothing. Never mind. I just hope the buses can get here soon."

Eddie nods. "If we're stuck here for a while, we could have lots of time to . . ."

His voice trails off, but I know what he's thinking. He wants to look around the house and find those secret inventions. "We should stay with the group. I know you have your blueprint and everything, but we already fell down a laundry chute."

"Sshh!" Eddie hisses, looking around. "The blueprint is our secret, right?"

"Sorry." No one pays any attention to us, though. "If there are inventions—they could be almost anything, right?"

"Exactly. That's why it's so fascinating. What if he invented a trampoline? But when you bounce, you bounce all the way into outer space. So you'd need to wear a space suit before you jumped on it or you'd suffocate since you can't breathe in space. Or what if he invented reusable toilet paper? That sounds horrible, right? But do you know how many trees are cut down every year to make toilet paper? Almost ten billion trees. So if it could be reused, like self-cleaning and reusable toilet paper that wasn't completely disgusting, that would be worth a fortune."

I just sit there, my mouth wide open. "Yeah. That would be, um, cool. Sure."

"What?" he asks, looking at my open mouth.

"Well . . ."

"Yes?"

"It's just that I don't know if those inventions are possible. I'm sure he created lots of epic things, but those ideas? Well, they don't make a lot of sense."

As soon as I say those words, Eddie stiffens. His eyes go wide and he coughs. His face turns slightly red. He crosses his arms and sniffs. "I was just kidding. There probably aren't any inventions, anyway."

"But maybe there are. What if we got all the kids to help look for them? What if we worked as a team? Like a platoon. If you showed everyone the blueprint—"

"No." Eddie interrupts me and frowns. "I told you to forget I have it. If there were inventions, I can find them without anyone's help."

"We all need help."

"Not me."

Just like that, Eddie sounds like the Eddie I see at school and who talked to me when we first became trip buddies—the Eddie who acts like he knows more than everyone. He lifts his nose a bit.

I sigh. I thought that Eddie was gone, but I was wrong.

I think it would be totally awesome to get everyone involved. When you work as a team, things get done. But a plan like that would need someone who can plan a strategy and get a team working together. It would need a leader.

As we sit, silent, other kids gab. They talk about the secret inventions mostly. Everyone's got crazy ideas.

"Maybe one of the inventions is a new smile," says Chloe. "For people who don't smile much. What do you think, Anna?"

"That would be nice," says Anna, but so quietly I can barely hear her.

"No, it wouldn't be nice at all," Sophie says, her voice dripping with scorn. "That would be dumb."

"You're right," says Chloe. "Sorry."

"Maybe he invented a nose picker," says Brian. "An automatic nose picker."

"Would it have a setting so you could eat boogers, too?" asks Seth.

"Of course," says Brian. "And when we find it—we'll get an A-plus on our essay."

"And no boogers, either!" Seth and Brian high-five each other: SMACK!

"You guys are gross," says Sophie.

Eddie listens, too. He doesn't look at anyone, he keeps his eyes fixed on his lap, but I can tell he listens by the way he shakes his head every time someone says anything. He mumbles, "I'm surrounded by people who make no sense."

I take a deep sigh, remembering the Eddie I saw just a few minutes ago—the Eddie who had invention ideas as bonkers as everyone else's ideas. I liked that Eddie. I hope he comes back soon.

Because I think *that's* the real Eddie. I just don't understand why he keeps pretending to be someone else.

18
JESSIE

Mr. St. Clare and Mr. Felix just passed out bowls of oatmeal and a piece of white bread to each of us. The oatmeal is one of the worst things I've ever eaten. I don't usually mind oatmeal, but I can barely eat this. I have to drink all my grape juice to get the taste out of my mouth. I don't eat much of it, so I'm still starving.

At least we had ketchup for the bread. It wasn't much, but it was better than nothing. They don't have butter.

Anna sits next to me, who sits next to Chloe, who sits next to Sophie. Anna stares at her legs, tears off part of her bread, and drops it on her lap.

That's just weird, but Anna is kooky anyway. I've never actually talked to her, but I can tell she's kooky. My cats can tell things, too, like if there's a dog outside even if it's not barking. And I'm very catlike.

The table grows quiet and I clear my throat. This is my

chance. I've been keeping a big secret all day, and now is the time to tell it. Mr. St. Clare is talking to Principal Klein in the far corner, and Mr. Felix disappeared as soon as he handed out the oatmeal.

I need to warn everyone about the robbery. Maybe someone can stop it.

"Listen up," I say. I lean in. "Hey, guys!" I speak louder, to get everyone's attention. The kids at my table look at me, but then I lower my voice again. "I need to tell you about Mr. St. Clare and Mr. Felix."

"That Mr. Felix guy gives me the creeps," says Brian.

"The double creeps," agrees Seth.

"Me too," I admit. "I heard him and Mr. St. Clare outside this morning. They were talking about stealing inventions and selling them for lots of money."

"Are you sure? That idea sounds as lame as this oatmeal," says Brian, pushing away his paper bowl.

I nod. "Yes, I'm sure. They even mentioned secret inventions. I'm not sure if they found them yet, but they're close. Just think how much money they'd get then."

"And they could get an A-plus if they wrote an essay," says Brian.

Eddie groans.

"Principal Klein says there are no secret inventions," says

Chloe. "And he's our principal so he would never lie. And Mr. Felix has been the groundskeeper almost his entire life. Why would he steal anything *now*?"

"I don't know, but I know what they said."

"You must have been hearing things," says Chloe.

"Maybe Mr. Minks invented something that makes you hear things," suggests Seth.

"I'd invent something that lets you hear farts," says Brian. "You know, the silent kind that smell the worst."

Everyone starts talking about secret inventions and ignores me. "I'm serious! Haven't you noticed all the half-empty rooms, and whenever anyone asks about it, Mr. St. Clare just changes the subject? Come on. We have to do something."

I might as well be talking to a wall.

But I know what I heard. I know what they are planning.

If no one believes me, I should stand up to Mr. Felix and Mr. St. Clare myself. And I would, if my cats were here. They would show those crooks they meant business.

Meanwhile, Chloe takes a small taste of oatmeal from her plastic spoon. "I think this is one of those things you have to get used to eating," she says. "Like coffee. I don't like coffee, but my mom says that when I'm older I'll drink it. Can you pass the ketchup?" she asks Anna.

"You're going to put ketchup in your oatmeal?" asks Sophie. "Gross!"

"Ketchup makes everything taste better," says Chloe.

"I doubt it will do any good," I warn.

Since I have the ketchup, Anna has to sit up to grab it. She could just ask me to pass it, but she doesn't. Instead, she leans way over. She does it awkwardly, with one hand sort of holding her stomach, so when she reaches over to me, she also knocks over her grape juice.

Her cup flops over and rolls away from her. A large trail of juice spreads across the white plastic tablecloth. The small purple river grows and flows past Chloe, inching farther and farther. Finally, it pours off the table and directly onto Sophie's lap.

Sophie jumps up and yelps. She sounds sort of like my house cat Oscar after I accidentally stepped on his tail once. Everyone in the dining hall stares at her. Sophie wears light yellow pants, so the giant stain of juice is impossible to miss. "What did you do?" Sophie screams.

Anna looks at Sophie, her eyes wide and her lips quivering. She drops the ketchup on the table. It lands on its side and some of it squirts out, blending into the grape juice. "S-Sorry."

"Are you kidding me?" asks Sophie, her voice loud and jarring. "You've ruined my favorite pants and all you can say is *sorry?*"

"It was an accident," Anna mumbles in her squeaky, quiet voice.

"Your whole life is a dumb accident!" shouts Sophie.

Anna's eyes fill with water. Her hands tremble. Fen sometimes jumps on the kitchen table at home and knocks things over. But do I get angry with him? Of course not. Fen is sensitive. Anna must be sensitive, too.

Sophie glares down at Anna. "I better be able to save these pants. If not, you're buying me a new pair. Come on, Chloe. Let's go to the bathroom and get away from this *accident*." She waves toward Anna but doesn't even look at her.

"Should I go, too?" asks Anna, her weak voice quaking. "Trip buddies are supposed to stay together."

"You think we're still trip buddies?" asks Sophie with a laugh. "I'd rather swim in an ocean of grape juice." Chloe still sits and Sophie pulls her arm. "Chloe? Earth to Chloe. Are you coming?"

"But doesn't Anna need a trip buddy?" Chloe asks. Her voice shakes, too. She looks at Anna and then at Sophie. The entire room looks at Anna and then at Sophie.

Chloe still doesn't stand up. Sophie taps her foot impatiently. "I said we're leaving, Chloe. Now." She points to the floor with a fierce jab.

Chloe stands up, bowing her head. "Yes, of course." To

Anna she says, "Sorry," and then hurries after Sophie, marching toward the bathroom.

Anna sits there, quivering. The entire room stares at her. You'd think people would feel sorry for her. She didn't spill that juice on purpose. But no. The way people stare and whisper, it looks like most of them are on Sophie's side.

I don't get it. Sophie is popular because she's mean to people, but being mean is a bad reason for someone to be popular. I think everyone just likes to go to her parties, even though she doesn't invite half the kids. She invited me last year, but I didn't go, because Fen was sick.

Meanwhile, Anna stares down at her lap. Tear dots are on her cheeks.

Would my cats like Anna? Sure, she mumbles and looks frumpy, but Patches likes dead mice. Maybe she sees something in dead mice that I don't see. Maybe there's something in Anna that I don't see.

Anna, still staring at her lap, picks up more tiny crumbs of her bread and sprinkles them on her lap again.

Anna must be nuts. My parents always tell me to wear a napkin on my lap during dinner so I keep crumbs off, and here she is, spreading them on her pants.

Then I hear a squeak.

I can't believe it, and I can't believe I didn't notice it

before now. Anna isn't putting crumbs on her lap because she's strange. She's feeding them to an animal hiding under her napkin.

It's a rabbit. I can see its nose and its whiskers.

Anna smuggled in a rabbit!

"What's her name?" I ask.

Anna looks up, her eyes wide and watery. "What?" Her voice is so quiet I can barely hear it.

"Your rabbit. Does it have a name?"

"Mopey. Her name is Mopey. But you can't say anything. Please. Not a word. I could get in trouble." She looks around, eyes wide, to make sure no one else is listening. But no one watches her now that Sophie has left the room. She talks so quietly no one would hear her anyway.

"I'm good at keeping secrets." I rub Mopey's head between the ears. Fen likes that. Mopey seems to like that, too. She purrs and squints. Fen does the exact same thing.

You know what? Maybe Anna isn't so bad. Anyone who would smuggle a rabbit on a trip can't be bad. "I need a trip buddy," I say to her. "Want to be mine?"

Anna wipes her nose with the back of her hand. She looks at me, as if waiting for me to make a joke.

"Please. You'd be doing me a big favor."

"Really?" Anna asks. I nod. "Okay, I mean if you really

need one." She smiles. It's a small smile and it lasts for just a second, but it's definitely a smile. Her eyes don't look quite so wet.

We both scratch Mopey between her ears. The rabbit snuggles against my hand, just like Fen does.

"Vivian and I are starting a club. It's called ART. It stands for Animals Rock, Totally! Maybe you should join. We're going to build an animal shelter in my backyard. We'll have cat food in it. And dog food. And snake food. Well, maybe not snake food. We're still working out the details."

"How about rabbit food?"

"Of course."

Anna smiles. "I'd like that. And you know, I believe you." I blink, confused. "About Mr. Felix and Mr. St. Clare. You said they want to steal stuff. I believe you."

"Thanks."

"And so does Mopey."

I scratch Mopey between the ears and she squints happily. I bet Mopey and my cats would all be best friends.

"What should we do about the thieves?" Anna asks.

"Just keep an eye out for anything suspicious, I guess," I say. "We can't do anything unless we catch them in the act. Otherwise, it's just our word against theirs. If the kids in our class won't listen, neither will adults."

Even though I feel sort of helpless to do anything, it feels good knowing someone believes me.

And you know what?

It feels good to have a trip buddy.

I know I want to be as independent as my cats, but I'm sure they'd enjoy having a trip buddy just as much as I do.

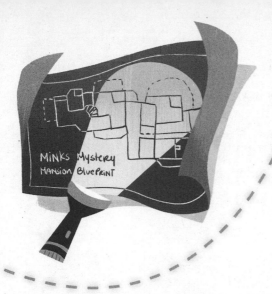

MINKS Mystery MANSION BluePrint

19
EDDIE

I finish all my oatmeal. Which was not easy. I think I'm the only kid who eats more than a bite.

It has a weird, lingering flavor. Like pickles, sort of. Yeah, that's it. Sour pickles.

Now that I think of it, the entire dining room sort of smells like pickles. It's not a nice smell, either.

I know I'm the great-great-great-grandson of Edward Minks, but I'm glad I don't truly have a bedroom in this house. There are way too many pickling things everywhere. I don't even like pickles.

In school, everyone seemed really interested that I was a Minks. I don't even know how Mrs. Greeley found out! My parents don't talk about it. I don't talk about it. It's sort of a family secret, I guess. My great-grandparents even changed our last name to Mudd so no one would know our history.

We've never wanted to admit that our family inherited nothing but a box of junk and some secrets that we didn't have a clue about.

But that box of junk had a house plan with clues. And those secrets are going to change my family's fortunes. My great-great-great-grandfather didn't leave us penniless, but with an opportunity.

It's an opportunity I can't let slip away.

Meanwhile, Mr. St. Clare huddles with Principal Klein.

"I'm sure they will be fine," says Mr. St. Clare as he and Principal Klein walk closer to our table.

"Mrs. Rosenbloom still hasn't answered my texts and this storm is simply horrible," says Principal Klein. "What if they are still outside? I should look for them. They might need my help."

"You can't go alone," says Mr. St. Clare. "Not in this weather, whether you want to or not. I'll go with you."

"Are you sure?" Principal Klein asks.

"I insist."

I pump my fist. This could be my chance. If they both leave, I'll be able to explore the house. Find the inventions. Claim our fortune.

"I know what you're thinking," says Aaron.

"What do you mean?"

"I heard the adults talking, too. I saw your fist pump. You

want to go off and explore the house. We should get everyone to help."

Of course Aaron would know my plan. But I can't have him tagging along. My dad says our family doesn't need anything from anyone. I mean, we're all Minkses. Or rather, we're all Mudds, but it's the same thing. "I don't need help."

"You could get lost," says Aaron. "I know it would be cool to find hidden inventions, but it's not worth the risk of getting lost or falling out a door and killing yourself just to get an A-plus on an essay."

"I don't care about getting an A-plus."

"Then what's going on? I don't get it. I know you told everyone you've been here all sorts of times, and you said you even have a bedroom here, but that's not true, is it? That's why you need the blueprint to find things. That's why you keep checking cracks and under stuff. You're looking for clues. It's okay. I know you haven't been telling me the truth. But I don't understand why. What's so important about finding those inventions, anyway?"

I open my mouth and then I close it again. I'm not sure what to say. I should have known Aaron would see through me. I take a deep breath.

He saved my life. He's been trying to help. He can help.

In a soft voice I say, "He left everything to the city, you

know. The Legend of Liberty Falls." I say those words as if they have a sour taste.

"So?"

"Who does that? I mean, my family got nothing. So, yes, I've never been here before. But if there are secret inventions, we inherit them. And then maybe things would be different."

"Like what?"

"Like maybe my parents would be happier. Maybe our house wouldn't be . . ." I stiffen. "Look, forget I said anything. I'm the great-great-great-grandson of Mr. Minks. It means I'm special, and way more special than anyone else." I lift my chin.

"I know you don't really mean that," says Aaron, shaking his head.

"Mean what?"

"I get it. It's your family's fortune. That's cool. But you're not fooling me. You're not as much of a jerk as you pretend to be sometimes."

I lower my chin. Aaron just doesn't understand. The bank isn't threatening to take away his family's house. Those inventions would solve all of our problems.

"And what if Jessie is right?" he asks. "What if there's a plot to steal the inventions? You don't want to get mixed up in that."

"I'm sure she's wrong."

"Probably, but if she's not . . ."

"I just need to figure out where that room is," I say, cutting Aaron off. If Mr. St. Clare and Mr. Felix are trying to steal my family's secrets, I'll just need to find those secrets first. "I've looked at my blueprint a zillion times. I thought that library clue was going to work. But I'm no closer than I was before we got here. But no one is as smart as me." Aaron frowns at me, and I know he hates it when I talk like that. "Sorry."

Aaron looks away, as if deep in thought. "Remember the sign in the lab?"

"Of course. It's famous:

Start work at 1

And you won't have any fun.

But start work at 01

And you'll have a ton!"

"It probably means something, right? It's so big, right?"

"His biggest poem ever. I thought it might mean something, too, but it's just a silly poem."

"I've been thinking. Maybe this isn't right, but my dad is in the army, and in the army, *zero one hundred* means one in the morning. So what if *start work at 01* refers to one a.m. army time?"

"Why didn't he write *01 hundred*?"

"It's a poem. Mr. St. Clare told us that nothing really rhymes with *hundred*, remember?"

"One sled," I say. "That rhymes."

"Yeah, well, that doesn't help. So maybe that sign is one giant clue. Maybe the hidden room is so secret it can only be found at one in the morning."

"Maybe." And maybe having someone help me isn't the worst thing in the world. I mean, Aaron has already thought of something I never did. "But if it can only be found at one a.m., how does that help? There are one hundred and twenty-four rooms in this place. I don't think we can be in one hundred and twenty-four rooms at the same time."

"We'll need to find more clues. We know the time. Now we just need to know the place."

"Sure. You're right. We'll find more clues." I lift up my chin. I'm a Mudd, or a Minks, or whatever. "I can find more clues without anyone else."

Aaron shakes his head at me.

I know I should stop doing that, and I should try harder to be a friend.

I want to be Aaron's friend.

But finding those inventions is the most important thing, and like my father says, we don't need anything from anyone. That fortune is the one thing that can help my family, and fortune is way more important than friendship.

20
CHLOE

Sophie and I return to the dining room from the bathroom, but instead of going to our table, we stand in the corner. We blotted and blotted, but Sophie didn't get the stain out. She stands next to me, half her pants purple and wet, staring at Anna.

I've seen Sophie angry, but never this angry. "We need to get even, we need to get even," she keeps saying.

"She didn't spill the drink on purpose," I say for the hundredth time.

"Stop saying that. You can't let people walk all over you. That's just dumb. And that *accident* isn't going to walk all over me. We need to get her and get her good."

She continues to glare at Anna with *that look*. It's an incredibly mean look, and I don't like it.

"She and Jessie aren't bothering anyone," I say.

Sophie growls at me. "You're either with me or against me. Are you my friend or not?"

I put my hands on my hips. "I'm your friend. You know that."

Some people say Sophie isn't always nice to people. I know that's true, but she stands up for herself, and that's a good thing. My mom says I need to stand up for myself more.

I think Sophie can be more like me, but I think part of me can be more like Sophie.

I bare my teeth and growl.

"What are you doing?" asks Sophie.

"Nothing. Sorry." I un-bare my teeth and smile. Growling doesn't feel right. I'm just not a Sophie, and I don't think I ever will be.

Principal Klein stares out the window, where snow continues to fall in buckets. "Let me call the school again and find out when the buses will be here," he says to Mr. St. Clare. "And then we'll look for Mrs. Rosenbloom and the students."

He fishes his phone from his pocket and then presses a few buttons. He puts it against his ear, and after a moment, he says, "Yes. Hi, Mrs. Frank, it's me." Mrs. Frank is our school secretary. "Fine, thank you. This storm has me worried . . . I'm sorry, I can barely hear you . . . You bought a duck? . . . Oh, you say they're stuck? . . . Nothing about ducks, then? . . . Our connection is bad, yes . . . Oh no—for how long? . . . Ping-Pong? Why would I talk about ducks playing Ping-Pong? . . . All night? Then you better call the parents . . . Hello? Mrs. Frank? Hello?" He lowers his phone and faces Mr. St. Clare. "A lot of static and then the line went dead. She said the roads are impassable. The buses are not going to make it here."

"Impassable?" says Mr. St. Clare. His face turns white. "So no vehicles can make it in. Are you sure? Nothing can get out, either?"

"No vehicles can drive on those roads tonight."

Mr. St. Clare bites his lips. "That is very bad news," he mutters, shaking his head.

"We're going to have to spend the night, I'm afraid. But we need to find the rest of my students. Can Mr. Felix keep an eye on things while we're outside? I hate to leave the kids alone in the house."

"Of course. I'll make sure he checks in on them while he's busy clearing out the inventions."

"Clearing out the inventions?" asks Principal Klein.

Mr. St. Clare coughs and looks away. "I mean, cleaning out the inventions. They get dirty. But we'll be back very soon. The kids will be fine under Mr. Felix's supervision."

I don't like the idea of Mr. Felix watching us, but I'm sure he's really nice and not as creepy as he seems—just like I'm super sure that all the kids from the other class are fine. Mrs. Rosenbloom is smart. You have to be smart to be a teacher. She probably found a quiet, cozy place for everyone to wait until the snow stops.

She was smart to miss dinner, anyway.

"I'm sure they'll be back soon," I say to Sophie.

She grunts. "Getting lost is dumb."

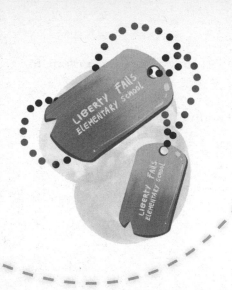

21
AARON

I sit with Eddie as Principal Klein and Mr. St. Clare prepare to leave. They put on their winter coats in the entryway.

"Did you know my great-great-great-grandfather built his first invention when he was just thirteen years old?" asks Eddie. I shake my head. "The Minks Magnificent Milking Machine could milk twenty cows at one time. He made a fortune. And then he became obsessed with inventing strawberry milk. He was convinced if he fed his cows nothing but strawberries every day, that would do it."

"Did it work?"

"Well, um, no. But even though he failed sometimes, he never stopped inventing. That's why he needed so much land and so many workers. He and Lady Minks—they were married by then—looked at lots of places to live. But every place they found had problems. Some places had giant bears. One place was infested with angry bees that had stingers three inches long! Finally, they found their way here. It was all wilderness back then, but they built the house and the factory and houses. And then Pickled Falls, or rather Liberty Falls, became famous."

"You know a lot about him, huh?"

"It is my legacy, right? My parents don't talk about him much. Neither do I. But my mom used to sing me a song at bedtime. I'm sure you know it."

And then, surprisingly, Eddie starts to sing to the tune of "Home on the Range."

Oh, give us a home where bears seldom roam
And bees won't sting us all day.
Where we can invent 100 percent,
And the trees will be shaped like sundaes.

Home, home in Liberty Falls!
We'll hang portraits of pickles on walls.
We'll never get bored of eating cardboard.
Let's just hope ghosts don't haunt the halls.

Oh, give us a town to turn the world upside down
And where pickling will always endure.
No one can outthink that inventing Minks—
He's the best! Well, top three for sure.

Home, home in Liberty Falls!
Don't get lost in its confusing halls.
You could call him cuckoo, but whatever you do—
Avoid Minks's pickled meatballs.

Eddie stops singing and looks at me. He must notice the blank look on my face. "You don't know the song?" I shake my head. "I thought everyone did."

"Kids, we're leaving now," announces Principal Klein. "The storm is not letting up. It may even be getting worse." He points out the window. All I can see is an ocean of white and the faint glow of a sunset. "While we're gone, you students should work on your essays. Yes, that would be a terrific idea. I'll collect those essays in the morning instead of next week."

Brian and Seth groan.

"Don't worry. We'll be back soon," says Mr. St. Clare. "Mr. Felix has already gathered pillows and blankets in the ballroom. Please do not wander around. As you know, it's easy to get lost in the mansion."

"You can count on us fifth graders," says Sophie.

"Such a good student," Principal Klein says.

"Mr. Felix has also set up an Invention Table," says Mr. St. Clare. "A rare treat. It's filled with many of the original tools Mr. Minks himself used. They are old and fragile, so please be gentle with them."

Principal Klein looks worried. "I know our fifth graders are very responsible, but if those tools are really old and fragile, do you think that's a good idea?"

Mr. St. Clare clears this throat. "Of course. Forget what I said. Students, please ignore the Invention Table. Pretend it's not there at all."

They turn to leave. I hope everyone out in the barn is fine. I'm sure they are. Still, that snow is coming down fast.

The front door opens, gusts of wind blow into the house, and then the door slams shut.

And just like that, we are alone.

22

JESSIE

We throw our paper bowls, plastic silverware, and plastic cups into garbage cans and then head to the grand ballroom. Outside, the snow continues to fall in the biggest flakes I've ever seen.

Mama says it rains cats and dogs, but that doesn't make sense, because cats look nothing like rain. But the snowflakes coming down now are almost cat-sized, so maybe people should say it snows cats and dogs. Or they could say it snows cats, because who needs a dog?

"I don't like snow," says Anna, cradling her rabbit under her frumpy brown sweater. "Neither does Mopey. She would be very scared if she were outside."

"My cat Oscar likes being outside."

"He must be brave."

I only wish I was as brave as Oscar. I don't like the idea of us being without an adult in this house. Though Mr. Felix is here, lurking somewhere and probably stealing things. At least with all this snow and the roads closed, he can't escape with those inventions. He's trapped here just like us.

Although being trapped in the same house as Mr. Felix doesn't make me feel much better.

We're not only trapped here with Mr. Felix, but we could also be trapped with ghosts! Everyone says this house is haunted. They say Mr. Minks roams the halls at night looking for things to pickle.

Mama says that when she was growing up in Beijing, she was told there are good ghosts and bad ghosts, but I don't want to see either kind. At home when I get scared at bedtime, my cats are there to protect me.

But who will protect me here?

As we enter the grand ballroom, I spy the Invention Table in the corner. It's a folding table covered in hammers and screwdrivers and nails. There are also blocks of wood and metal gears. A lot of it looks rusted.

I'm glad Mr. St. Clare told us to leave that stuff alone. It looks dangerous and fragile.

I walk over to the pile of pillows and blankets in the corner. Anna and I grab one of each and walk to the side of the room to set up our beds. Then we sit and pet Mopey's fur.

"I think Mopey is hungry," says Anna. "He didn't eat most of the bread."

"I bet everyone is hungry. No one ate very much at dinner. Maybe we can find food in the kitchen?"

Anna opens her backpack and slides Mopey inside a small cage. I wondered why her backpack was so enormous! "She likes it in here," says Anna, and partially zips the bag.

"Do you bring her to school every day?" I ask.

Anna shakes her head. "This backpack won't fit in my locker. It's only good for field trips." Then we stand up and walk back into the dining room.

We get to the doors that lead to the kitchen.

I push them open.

The kitchen is huge, with dozens of cabinets and a giant sink with twelve faucets. Everything feels really old. It even smells old, like wood and dust. There's also a nasty sour pickle smell coming from somewhere.

We open drawers and doors, but all we find is an empty tub of oatmeal and some paper plates. Anna opens the refrigerator, but there's nothing inside it.

I pull open a cabinet. "Hey, I found something." Inside are a bunch of small pink boxes that are each labeled *Instant Scrambled Egg Breakfast with Blueberry Muffin Cardboard Dessert*. I remove a box and shake it. There's nothing inside. "No eggs, but how horrible can blueberry muffin cardboard be?" I tear off a small sliver of the box and put it into my mouth.

I guess blueberry muffin cardboard can be pretty horrible. It tastes like soggy cardboard mixed with rotten blueberries and gym socks. I immediately spit it out. "I wouldn't feed this to a dead mouse."

"That bad?" asks Anna.

"It would be better than starving. But barely."

"Maybe it tasted better a hundred and fifty years ago."

"I doubt it." I stand there, frowning. I take a deep sniff. That sour pickle stink seems stronger. I follow my nose across the kitchen to a pantry we haven't open. It's the only door we haven't open.

I put my hand on the knob, hold my breath, and yank.

I'm hit with a horrible pickle-and-sour-fish stench coming from a large barrel. When I look at it, I have to turn away. Fen would hate this. I'm so glad he isn't here. "That smell is so horrible it probably even keeps ghosts away."

"What is it?" Anna asks.

"I think it must be pickle juice. Mr. St. Clare mentioned they keep a barrel for experiments." Above the barrel is a shelf, and on the shelf is a jar filled with shriveled, brownish pickles. "Those must be one-hundred-and-fifty-year-old pickles."

"Can we please leave?" asks Anna, holding her breath.

I close the door and we hurry away, out of the kitchen.

"I just hope we can get out in the morning," says Anna. "Poor Mopey will be hungry. We could be trapped here for days."

Days? I hadn't thought of that. We always can eat the cardboard if we're desperate enough. But what if my sister forgets to feed my cats while I'm away? What if Mrs. Rosenbloom and the missing kids are never found? What if Mr. Felix starts snipping his hedge clippers at us and keeps us prisoners while he steals everything in the house?

"We'll be fine," I say. I smile, because if Anna knew how nervous I really was, we'd both be screaming as loud as we could.

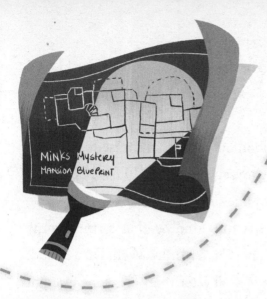

23
EDDIE

As soon as the door closes and Principal Klein and Mr. St. Clare are gone, it hits me.

I'm alone.

I mean, I'm not *alone* alone. There are still lots of kids here. But we have no adults watching us. We have no one to tell us what to do, no one to make sure we don't break any rules.

Most importantly, there's no one to stop me from using my blueprint to hunt for that secret invention room. If Jessie is right about things, Mr. Felix could be looking for it right now!

I need to find it first.

I sit in the corner of the room and open my blueprint. My fingers shake. This is my chance.

My family's future could change tonight.

I'll study the blueprint one last time, and then I'm out of here.

"It's not safe to sneak around the house alone, you know," says Aaron. He throws two pillows and two blankets next to me and sits on the floor.

I'm surprised to see Aaron but also not surprised. I want to look at the blueprint all by myself. But I would have been disappointed if Aaron hadn't joined me.

Still, the blueprint is not his. Finding that fortune is my responsibility. I like Aaron, but I'm a Minks. Well, I'm a Mudd. But us Minkses and Mudds are better than everyone else put together. As my dad says, we don't need anyone.

"I'm not going to sneak anywhere," I say. "We were told to wait in the ballroom."

"Because even with your blueprint, it's easy to get lost," says Aaron.

"I totally and absolutely agree."

There's a loud RING followed by a CLANK and a BZZZZZ!

I wheel around. Brian rummages around the Invention Table. "Look at this!" he yells. He holds some sort of tool that looks like the top of a hammer attached to part of a screwdriver attached to some pliers.

"We were told not to touch any of that stuff," lectures Chloe.

"Leave it alone," Aaron says.

"Fine. Never mind," says Brian with a frown. He slams the tool down on the table, and the table cracks in half.

CRNKLLEEZZXX!!

Everything falls on the floor. Metal and glass shatter, wood splinters, something sparks, and a cloud of dust shoots up into the air. A thousand tiny objects spark and sizzle. "Whoops," says Brian.

I groan. Brian has just ruined a whole bunch of priceless antiques.

Something hard hits my shoulder. "Ow!" I look down and pick up an eraser that just hit me.

"Got you!" yells Seth, cradling an armful of erasers. "Who wants to play Eraser Wars?" He hurls another eraser toward me, but it sails over my head.

I heard Brian and Seth invented a game called Eraser Wars. It's a game where you throw erasers at each other. It's just another thing that makes no sense from kids who make no sense.

"I'm in!" yells Brian, jogging over from the Invention Pile of Broken Stuff that used to be the Invention Table.

At least he and Seth can't do any damage throwing erasers.

CRAZZZSH!

An eraser bounces off a pickled-food picture hanging on the wall. The portrait hangs awkwardly on the wall, shakes a little, and then falls. The glass shatters as it hits the ground. The frame breaks in half.

"Whoops," says Seth.

At least, I didn't think they could do any damage with erasers.

I scan the group. Jessie and Anna huddle together. Norm and Wesley whisper to each other and point to the staircase.

But I can't sit here watching my classmates and ducking erasers. I need to find those inventions. The adults could be back any time.

With my blueprint in my hand, I stand up. I'll start on the second floor and work my way up.

"I thought you weren't going to sneak around with your blueprint," says Aaron.

"Just a quick look. No worries."

"Then I should go with you," says Aaron.

I shake my head. "I'm going alone."

"But we can get everyone to help," says Aaron. "You should ask everyone to look. Teamwork, you know? Like an army platoon."

An eraser hits Aaron on the head. While he's distracted, I march out of the room and dash toward the stairs. Aaron doesn't follow me.

The first place I'm going is up that gloomy staircase behind the painting of the gloomy staircase. I bet those secret inventions are somewhere up there. I bet that's why Mr. St. Clare didn't want us to go up those stairs.

As I take the first step up the grand stairway, I stop. Am I making a mistake? Is walking around the house by myself something that makes no sense?

No. I'm a Minks. A Mudd. A Mudd-Minks. And I always make perfect sense.

24

CHLOE

Lots of kids are missing, and I'm not just talking about the ones who went to the barn this morning.

I don't see Eddie or Brian or Seth. I don't see Wesley and Norm, either. They are wandering around and are just asking for trouble. We were told to stay put, and we should stay put.

Sophie digs into her backpack and pulls out a granola bar. I look inside her backpack. She must have twenty granola bars in there! "Where did you get those?"

"Sshh!" Sophie puts a finger over her lips. She talks in a near whisper. "I overheard Mr. St. Clare say that he kept a secret stash in the closet. Well, he used to. They are mine now. But keep it a secret." She unwraps the bar and takes a bite.

My stomach growls. I watch Sophie bite into her bar. "Can I have one?"

"Too risky. Someone might see."

"But you're eating one," I say, my mouth frowning and my stomach grumbling.

Sophie pops the rest of the bar into her mouth and quickly swallows it. "Not anymore," she wheezes, coughing.

I cross my arms. If I had bars, I'd share them with Sophie. I'd share them with everyone. "We're all hungry. None of us ate very much at dinner."

"That's not my problem. I'll give you one later. We should work on our essays now. We're all supposed to write essays, remember?"

I nod, although I'm still annoyed. I unzip my backpack and remove a notebook and a pencil. Sophie doesn't move.

"I thought we were going to work on our reports," I say.

"I can't reach my pencil. There are too many granola bars in the way. You write one, and I'll just copy it and give you a granola bar. That sounds fair. A report for a granola bar."

"You said you'd give me a granola bar anyway."

"This way is better."

I grit my teeth. Part of me wants to demand that Sophie should write her own essay and give me a granola bar. Now! And she should share her granola bars with everyone.

But I don't say anything. I'm not tough like Sophie. And while it's not nice to hide granola bars, they are hers and not mine. Maybe she'll change her mind and share later.

As I open my notebook, Sophie pulls another bar out of her backpack and unwraps it. She takes a bite.

"I thought it was too risky to eat another one now," I protest.

Sophie puts the rest of the bar in her pocket. "No one was looking, but we can't take the chance again."

I grumble and try not to think about food as I start to write. But what should I write about?

We've learned so much.

I could write about how Minks wanted to make the world a better place. I could write about how he never gave up, even when he failed.

I remember two summers ago. I tried out for a new dance team. Before tryouts, the teacher told us, "We can't take everyone. If you don't make it, I hope you'll continue to dance and try out again next year."

I made the team, but lots of girls didn't. I thought I'd see them at tryouts this year, but none of those girls came back. I bet they gave up. That's what made Mr. Minks so wondertastic. He never stopped trying. He didn't let one setback keep him down. I think that's a great lesson for everyone.

I bet some of those girls would have made the dance team if only they had tried and tried again. I bet Mr. Minks would have made our dance team if he had tried out again! I bet he'd be the best dancer on our team! I bet he'd invent a new kind of dance shoe and funtastic new tutus.

"What are you doing?" asks Sophie.

I look up from my page. "What?"

She's looking over my shoulder and reading my report. "You're writing about dancing. I'm not a dancer and neither was Mr. Minks. And why would he be dancing on a fifth-grade dance team? Dancing is dumb. How am I supposed to copy a report about dancing?"

"You're right," I say. "I wasn't thinking." I tear the page out of my notebook and crumble it up. "I'll start over. I'll write about some of the inventions we've seen."

Sophie sighs and then points to Anna and Jessie. They sit together talking. But now that I look closer, I think they might be petting something, too. "What are they doing?" Sophie asks.

"Playing with Soda, the hamster, maybe?" Kyle probably left her behind so Jessie and Anna could keep her company. That was super nice of him.

I'm about to suggest we pet Soda, too, because she's so cuddly and soft, but then I remember that Sophie doesn't like hamsters.

Sophie shakes her head. "No, that thing is bigger than Soda." Her eyes widen. She stares and stares. "I think it's a rabbit."

"Are you sure?" I crane my neck, but I can't see what they are petting. "Where would they get a rabbit?"

Sophie's eyes blaze. "I don't know. Let's grab it. We can hide it."

"What? Why would we do that?" Rabbits are even cuter than hamsters.

"Hello? Earth to Chloe? Anna ruined my pants, remember?" The liquid has dried, but Sophie's pale yellow pants still have a big purple stain. "She has to pay."

"Let's leave them alone."

Sophie glares at me. "You're either with me or against me. Are you my friend or not?"

I should stand against her. If we're such best friends, then why didn't Sophie share a granola bar with me? I look in her eyes. I curl my fingers into determined fists. I sit up straight.

And then I sigh and open my hands and look down at the floor. "I'm with you, of course." I sit up straight again. I have an idea. "I know. Instead of taking the rabbit, we could take Anna's pillow." That seems mean, too. The floor is hard. I don't think I could sleep without a pillow.

"Take her pillow? What sort of revenge is that?" She looks upset with me.

"Never mind," I say, and my shoulders sag.

Then Jessie and Anna put the rabbit into Anna's giant

backpack, stand up, and march out of the room and into the dining room.

"Well, look at that," says Sophie. She rubs her hands together and smiles. "This is our chance."

"How about if we look at the rabbit first?" I rub my best friend necklace, the one that matches Sophie's, although Sophie doesn't wear hers anymore. I know Sophie won't want to take the rabbit once she sees how cute it is. Sophie may act mean, but deep down she's super nice, at least I think she must be. She just needs to be reminded of it, and a cute, cuddly rabbit could wipe the mean from anyone.

After playing with the rabbit, I'll be eating a granola bar. I'm sure everyone will be eating one.

"Whatever. I'm still taking it," she growls.

We walk over to Anna's backpack, which is unzipped. Now I know why Anna was lugging such a huge backpack. Inside is a small cage with her rabbit. I carefully open the gate and lift out the animal.

It's so soft and cuddly—even cuddlier than I thought. Sophie shrinks away, as if I'm holding a snake or something.

"Go ahead," I say. "Pet her."

"I've petted an animal before," she says, rolling her eyes. I continue holding the rabbit out. She throws me an angry look, but then she touches the rabbit. Just a quick touch. Then she touches the rabbit again. Soon she's scratching it. "I guess it's soft."

"See? Rabbits are funtastic."

"It's not completely horrible. Whatever." I hand Sophie the rabbit. She jerks her arms away, but I continue holding the rabbit out until Sophie takes it from me. She grabs it a little awkwardly but then sits down and rests it on her lap. "Fine. You're right. It's sort of cute. And I guess hiding it would be dumb."

"I bet your baby brother would like rabbits, too."

Sophie frowns at me, but then her frown turns into a smile. "I think he would. Maybe my parents will get one for him."

I grin. It's great seeing the nicer side of Sophie again. This is the Sophie who is my best friend, not that mean Sophie who pops out most of the time.

There's a loud creak from the side of the room. I'm not sure what it is, maybe just an old-house sound, but Sophie jumps up, startled. "Ghosts?"

"It's nothing," I say.

But when Sophie jumps up, the rabbit slides to the floor. It must be scared, because it races away.

"Hey!" shouts Sophie.

She runs after Anna's rabbit, and I run after them.

But the rabbit is fast. Much faster than I think it should be. It scampers across the room, where it heads toward an open vent.

If it gets in that vent, we might never find it.

Sophie dives forward, her arms outstretched.

Just as the rabbit steps into the vent, Sophie grabs one of its back legs. "Got it!"

She tugs the rabbit toward her. She clutches the animal in her hands. "It's all right," she whispers to it. "Everything is fine now." She strokes the rabbit's back.

My heart is beating like a zillion times a second. Sophie looks just as panicked as I feel. "We better put it back in its cage, before Jessie and Anna get back," I say.

"Good idea."

I hear footsteps.

Anna and Jessie walk back into the room, just like that. I'm not sure where they went, but we have their rabbit, and I don't know how to explain why we're holding it, without admitting we took it from Anna's backpack.

Sophie dashes over to our gear, grabs her backpack, and stuffs the rabbit inside it. She zips it up, but leaves enough open so the animal can breathe. She puts her finger over her lips. "Sshh."

Then Anna calls out in a panicked voice, "Where's Mopey? Help!"

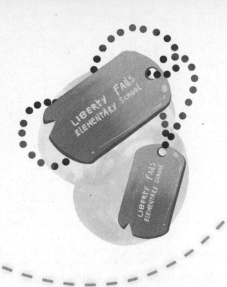

25
AARON

I should never have let Eddie go looking around alone.

Sure, Eddie has that blueprint, but the house is still ginormous and confusing, and the blueprint doesn't show everything. It doesn't show most things.

Whenever my family moves to a new place, I sneak off and explore places like cool old, abandoned buildings or small bike paths. I'm not a chicken, because I always know my way back.

But there's something about this house—something that gives me the jitters. I worry that if we split up from the group we'll fall down a hole that doesn't lead to a laundry room but into a dungeon.

My dad wouldn't have let his trip buddy wander off. He would have served and protected. Maybe being all I can be, like my dad says I should be, doesn't just mean being a good soldier. Maybe it means you have to be a sergeant or a general sometimes. Take charge. Lead the team.

And tell your trip buddy to chill out.

I look up when someone yells, "Mopey is missing!" It's Anna, and she's throwing her pillow and covers. "Help me! Help me!" I've never heard her speak louder than a whisper. I didn't think she could speak louder than a whisper. "Help!"

I guess she can yell pretty loudly when she wants to. She nearly sobs between shouts.

"What's a Mopey?" I ask.

"Her rabbit," says Jessie, tossing her own pillow and blanket to the side, looking.

"You brought a rabbit?" someone else asks.

"Everyone! Please!" hollers Jessie. "Focus. We need to find Anna's rabbit. She's lost."

Back at my dad's last army base in Alaska, we had a dog. It wasn't my own personal dog, but the army base's dog. Everyone took care of Bernie, but he played with me the most. He was a black Labrador-collie mix, which, if you ask me, is the coolest dog on the planet.

One day, Bernie jumped over a fence and got lost, and the entire platoon spent half the day looking for him. We found him trapped under a bridge. He was caught in some plastic, I think from a pop six-pack. He was fine, but it was one of the worst days of my life.

So I know how worried Anna must be. I hope Mopey isn't caught on something.

Everyone in the room looks through their gear. We're all a team now. A platoon, working together. As I gaze around the room, I feel a lump in my throat, because I can't stop thinking of Bernie.

Except. Wait a second.

Not everyone looks for Mopey.

Chloe isn't searching. Neither is Sophie. They both sit in the corner. They both shake their heads and stare at the ground.

Dad says that in the army, you always need to be on the lookout for things that seem wrong.

Sophie just seems wrong. Always. Chloe seems wrong right now, too.

"She could be lost forever!" Anna wails.

I take a deep breath, and I march over to Sophie. It's time I was a general or a sergeant. It's time for me to be all that I can be.

Sergeants and generals bark at people. People listen to them. "Atten-*shun*, Private! Did you take her?"

"What did you call me?" asks Sophie.

I ignore her question. I guess adding *private* was a bit too much. "Do you know where Mopey is?"

Sophie shakes her head. "Who?" She smiles like she does around adults sometimes, and I know she's fibbing. I guess I don't make a great sergeant. I should have had someone else bark at them. I'm not a leader.

But while Sophie is a good liar, Chloe is not. She shivers and sits with her hands wrapped around her knees. She doesn't look at me. She acts guilty.

"Give her back." I say this loudly, maybe a bit too loudly, but sergeants talk loudly.

Other kids notice. Anna and Jessie approach us. Jessie is mostly nice, but she can look tough when she wants to, and right now she looks really tough. Anna is almost shaking with worry, but Jessie is steady. Steady and tough.

"Do you know where Mopey is?" asks Jessie, her voice firm and slightly scary and I think she would make a way better sergeant than me.

"What's it to you?" Sophie asks.

"If you took her, I swear . . ." Behind Jessie, Anna bites her fingernails.

"She's fine," says Chloe, her voice quakes. "She's right . . ."

"In the mansion," interrupts Sophie. "Somewhere. We saw where it went. It's safe. For now."

"Where is she?" asks Anna, shaking.

Sophie breaks into a grin. "I'll tell you under one condition."

"Anything!" pleads Anna.

Sophie smiles wider. "Anything?" Anna nods. "Okay, I'll tell you what. I'll tell you—but you have to go into the basement. Alone."

Everyone in the room gasps. I gasp just as loud.

Nothing much frightens me, but all basements are a little scary. I remember the stairway light is broken. Walking down that staircase alone would be bonkers. It creaks and moans and . . .

And then Anna says what we're all thinking. She says it in her tiny whisper of a voice. "But what if there are ghosts down there?"

Sophie shrugs. "Don't go, then. Good luck finding your rabbit, though."

If there are ghosts, I'm sure they hang in the basement. I wouldn't go into that basement alone, even if I were a sergeant or general.

"I have a better offer for you," says Jessie, making a fist.

"Stop," says Anna, her voice struggling to break through the tiniest of whispers. She grabs Jessie's arm. "I don't like fighting. I'll go."

Sophie smiles. It's sort of a nasty smile. "When you come up, I'll show you where your rabbit is. If the ghosts don't get you first."

"I'm going with her," says Jessie.

"I'm supposed to go b-by m-myself," whimpers Anna. Her hands shake.

I should go with Anna. Dad would go with her. Army guys do that sort of thing. They aren't scared of ghosts.

But before I can offer, Sophie says, "That's a better idea.

You both should go. But you have to be down there for ten minutes. Not a second less."

I'm glad I don't have to volunteer to go, but I wish I didn't feel that way.

"I'm sorry about your rabbit," Chloe says, but the words barely come out of her mouth. She sort of chokes them out.

"You are so lame," Sophie says to Chloe.

Chloe hangs her head.

Anna and Jessie walk toward the basement door.

"That's what she gets for spilling punch on me," Sophie says to Chloe, just loud enough so I hear it, too.

26

JESSIE

Anna and I head down the dark basement stairs. One step, two steps. We can't walk too fast or we could fall. The dark staircase was only a little scary when we were with our entire group. But it's really, really scary with just the two of us.

I read somewhere that cats can see ghosts. If they do, they're even braver than I can imagine, because my cats go down to our basement all the time.

I never go into our basement at home unless I'm with one of my cats.

The stairs creak and moan. I grab the handrail, but it's sticky and scratchy, so I let go.

"D-Do you think we'll see ghosts?" stutters Anna.

"Of course not," I say, trying to sound brave and ignoring the shivers racing up and down my back.

Below us, each creak sounds sort of like a ghost moan.

I stumble as my foot hits the bottom step, because I'm

expecting another step, but instead it's the floor. I put my hand on the wall to steady myself. Cracks rumble from the wall.

"What's that?" asks Anna. I can feel her shaking behind me. The floor shakes a little, too.

"It's just the wall," I say. "Basements and walls make funny noises sometimes."

It takes all my nerve not to turn around and run back up the stairs, but then Anna might not get Mopey back. Anna thinks I'm brave, but that's because she doesn't know the real me, only the pretend me.

Upstairs, when I spoke up to Sophie, I tried to act tough. But I would never fight anyone, not really! I thought if I acted tough, Sophie would give us Mopey back.

But instead I'm in a scary basement, so that didn't work out at all.

I move my hand, and it hits a light switch. I have never been so happy to see light.

Things don't seem as frightening when there's light.

Mama says there is nothing in the dark that's not in the light. Maybe. But it's much easier to hide in the dark, so you never know what might be ready to jump out at you.

When we build our Animals Rock, Totally! animal shelter, I'll make sure there's a night-light in it so animals don't get scared. Not all animals are as brave as cats.

We step forward, and the floor creaks again.

"Wh-What was that?" Anna bites her nails.

"It's just the floor," I say, keeping my voice steady.

Now that the lights are on, the color yellow surrounds us. I'm glad the room is yellow, because yellow is sort of the color of an ocicat, although we don't have that cat breed at home because Mama refuses to get any more cats.

"Don't forget about the ghost trap," I say, pointing to the net under the pool table.

We stay clear of the pool table.

I sit on the large yellow couch. It's leather and comfy and makes a grumbling sound.

"What was that?" Anna asks, trembling.

"Just the sofa."

"Do you think it's been ten minutes yet?"

"I think it's only been about thirty seconds."

I sit. Anna stands. Neither of us wears a watch. I count seconds in my head. Two minutes. Three minutes.

The floor squeaks.

"Who's there?" asks Anna, her knees knocking.

"It's just more old-house sounds. Everything's fine."

Something breathes above us.

"Is that a ghost?" whispers Anna, shaking.

"I think it's the air vent."

I remind myself there are no ghosts. It's just Anna and me. I'm being silly.

It's just us.

Just us.

My mind wanders. I look down the hallway. I can see the door leading to the laundry room.

"If we go up now, do you think Sophie will tell us where Mopey is?" Anna asks.

"Let's wait another couple of minutes, just to be sure." I'm not convinced Sophie will give Mopey back if we stay down here for an hour. I don't trust her. She says she knows where Mopey is, which either means she's lying or she nabbed Mopey.

And I'm pretty sure she nabbed Mopey.

And maybe Chloe helped. Chloe acts nice most of the time, but someone who would help steal a rabbit can't be nice at all.

As I sit, my eyes stay focused on the hallway. "Hold on." I have an idea. "We can't let Sophie get away with this. We need to do something." And I know exactly what that something should be. "Where do you think we can find a Magic Marker?"

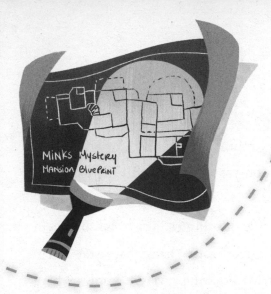

My blueprint shows a door in this hallway that leads to a supply room. Supply rooms are filled with things. Some of those things could be secret inventions.

But there is only a wall in front of me.

I turn the blueprint upside down. Maybe I'm looking at it wrong.

No, that doesn't help.

Or I need to go in the door across the hall. Yes, that must be it. I've just reversed things.

I walk a few steps farther and stop in front of a painting of a bright stairway. I push it and find a bright stairway. There's a big window in the stairwell, and moonlight manages to shine through despite all the snow swirling outside.

There are lots of stairways in this place, but I can't find this one in my plans. Maybe I'm in the wrong hall?

Did I turn left after the Chilly Chamber or right?

I can't remember. I'm all twisted and turned.

The Chilly Chamber is famous. As we learned in school, my great-great-great-grandfather thought preserving food was really important. He wanted to help lots of people by making fresh food last longer. So he not only pickled things but tried refrigerating them. He built an entire room that would stay cold forever, as long as you kept an ice cube in the corner of the room. It was quite a breakthrough. He imagined a Chilly Chamber in every house.

But the room needed extra-thick and heavy insulation to stay cold, and the insulation weighed more than three hundred tons. After he finished building the room, it crashed through the floor and into the basement, where the insulation exploded.

The Chilly Chamber crashed through this mansion five times before my great-great-great-grandfather built a floor strong enough to hold it. It also exploded twice.

Before my great-great-great-grandfather could work out all the problems, electric refrigerators were invented, and three-hundred-ton exploding refrigeration rooms weren't needed.

When I was in the chamber, I didn't think it was very chilly, though. Surprising. I read the same ice cube has been used to freeze the room for one hundred years, and the room is always kept at exactly zero degrees.

But I couldn't find the ice cube. It was almost as if someone had taken it.

I'm as lost now as the ice cube. Maybe I left the Chilly Chamber from a different door than the one I entered. There were two doors. But then when I walked out that door, which way did I turn? Left? And then there was that tall and thin staircase, behind the painting of a tall, thin staircase. I climbed those and turned right.

Or did I turn left again?

And where is that staircase, because I didn't see it on the blueprint, and now I can't remember. Is it back down the hallway? Maybe I should turn around.

I have no idea where I am. I might be on the fifth floor, or the third floor, or the seventh floor. There is a door with a picture of a wall in front of me. When I open it, there are more stairs. I don't know. Maybe if I climb these, I'll figure out where I am on this blueprint.

I climb, but as I do, the ceiling gets closer and closer to me, and pretty soon I have to walk on my knees, and then the stairs end at a wall. I should have figured that would happen from the painting. I need to turn around, which isn't easy in such a crammed stairwell. I have to inch backward until I have enough space to stand and walk back down.

Then I turn left and open a door with a picture of a giant icicle on it, and I'm back inside the Chilly Chamber.

This is the most confusing house ever.

I walk across the room and leave through a totally different door, and now I'm in a hallway I haven't seen before. "Help!" I scream, but I'm screaming to myself, because no one is around.

I should have brought Aaron with me. I should have trusted him more. If I ever find my way back to the ballroom, I'll let him find stuff with me.

He's my friend. Well, maybe he's my friend. No, he is.

Friends tell each other stuff. Maybe I'll tell him things I've never told anyone, like how my dad hasn't had a job in six months and that if I don't find these inventions, we might lose our house.

I push open a door without a painting on it. If I push open enough doors, one of them will have hidden inventions, right? Maybe this is it right here.

It's just a closet.

I close the door.

I study the blueprint.

But continuing to look at something that doesn't make sense also makes no sense.

I should give up and admit there aren't any secret inventions. Dogs have searched the house, detectives have searched the house, people with metal detectors have searched the house, and once, some sort of famous mystic searched the house.

If none of them could find a secret room with secret inventions, why did I think I could find them, even with my blueprint?

I thought I was smarter than everyone else. I was wrong. Maybe I don't make any more or less sense than anyone else. And maybe just because I'm a Minks doesn't mean I don't need help. Maybe we all need help, at least sometimes.

The hallway in front of me is lined with small lights that stick out from the walls. Each is shaped like a pickle. I groan. If I never see a pickle again after this trip, I'll be happy.

I grab the pickle light closest to me. It's a little bigger than the other pickle lights. I'm so frustrated, I want to rip it off the wall.

But it doesn't rip off, it moves.

And a hidden door, which was right next to me but was nearly impossible to see because it just looked like part of the wall, opens.

I hold my breath as I step inside the room. This could be it—the secret room no one has ever found!

I release my breath. This is not a secret room that no one has seen for 150 years. Actually, this looks like a room that's used often, and recently. It's an office, with filing cabinets and a desk, and on the desk is a mug that says THIS MUG IS HALF EMPTY on it, and a bunch of pens and pencils, and a large notepad.

There are also maps taped all over the wall.

These aren't maps of other countries like in our classroom at school, or road maps like from the Minks Mystery Mansion library. These are hand-drawn maps of the house and the land around it. I see rooms I don't recognize and hallways that don't match my blueprint. Some rooms are circled with notes like *Ignore this room* and *Remove the invention here.*

One note on a map points to the inventor's workshop we saw this morning, and says, *Take everything but the paste.*

A map of the failed inventions room reads, *Take everything on the left side of the room.*

And yet another map shows the Chilly Chamber I was just in. A note on it says, *Take the ice cube.*

When Jessie said she overhead Mr. St. Clare and Mr. Felix talking about stealing inventions, I truly hoped she was wrong. I hoped she wasn't making any sense.

But it looks like she made complete sense, and this is the proof. It's even worse than I feared.

One of the maps on the wall shows the lawn in the front of the house and the word *HOLES* in all caps at the top. There are big *X*s drawn everywhere with the word *No* written next to each one.

No. No. No. No. No. No. No. No. No. No. No. No. No. No. No.

What if they weren't digging holes for moles but for buried treasure? Maybe the secret inventions are buried underground.

If they were, it appears Mr. St. Clare and Mr. Felix didn't find anything.

I look down at the desk and the notepad on it. A series of numbers with dollar signs are written down. The numbers range from a few thousand dollars to tens of thousands of dollars. If I added them all up, they would add up to a fortune.

At the end of the page, someone wrote:

These are low-end numbers. We should expect more money. A lot more.

I continue flipping through the notepad. My hands are trembling. There are scribbles and lots of handwriting. I can't read most of it, but there are also drawings of inventions. Some inventions I recognize, and some I don't.

There's a sketch of the Minks Magnificent Milking Machine—my great-great-great-grandfather's first invention— and a doodle of the Minks Wonderful Workout Washer we saw in the basement. Next to that drawing is a note: *Too big. Leave it here.*

I need help. "Hello?" I yell out. "Anyone?"

But then I stop yelling.

What if Mr. Felix hears me? He could be lurking any-where. He could be coming to this room any second.

And what about Mr. St. Clare? Is he still outside looking for the missing students, or has he taken Principal Klein hostage? What if all the missing kids are locked in a room somewhere?

What if the kids in this house are next to be captured?

I'm alone, lost, and I can't do anything to warn anyone or stop anything.

My great-great-great-grandfather didn't leave my family those inventions. I shouldn't care if they are stolen.

But I do care.

Odd.

Maybe a legacy isn't only about money but about his-tory and the knowledge you leave behind. Maybe my great-great-great-grandfather's wish to "profit the world" makes sense.

I don't know if I can find secret inventions. But I can try to stop Mr. Felix and Mr. St. Clare from stealing ones that aren't hidden.

I rush out of the room, down the hall, and try another door with a painting of zigzagging lines on it. It just leads to a hallway, a hallway that zigzags back and forth. My heart is pounding. I hope this hallway leads somewhere that can get me back to the ballroom.

I can't stop them alone. I need help, and I need to get back.

28
CHLOE

Mopey is tucked away in Sophie's luggage, the zipper open a crack so she can breathe.

"If that rabbit goes to the bathroom in there, I'm flushing it down the toilet," says Sophie. "That's what my parents did to my fish."

I don't think a rabbit would fit in a toilet, but I just smile and hope Mopey doesn't go to the bathroom. I think Sophie is just kidding anyway. At least I hope she's joking.

"I thought you liked rabbits," I say. "You said you might even ask your mom for one. Your baby brother would like it."

"I didn't say that."

"Sure you did."

Sophie shakes her head. "Rabbits are dumb. And so are baby brothers."

As Sophie grumbles to herself, I can't get the big lump out of my throat. We should have returned Mopey to Anna, and we shouldn't have sent Anna and Jessie to the basement. I should have said something. I should have stood up for them.

For a moment, when she was petting Mopey, I thought the nicer Sophie had returned, the one I loved hanging out with. I was wrong.

My uncle was sick a few years ago, and Sophie visited me every night to cheer me up, which was nice. We did our homework together and told jokes. That's the Sophie I liked. That's the nice Sophie.

Although, now that I think about it, it was mostly me doing the homework and Sophie telling the jokes, so maybe Sophie wasn't being all that nice.

She's my best friend. She's been my best friend for as long as I can remember. But does that mean she should be my best friend forever? Best friends share granola bars. Best friends help each other with homework. Best friends are nice to each other.

"WooOOOooOOOooo!!!"

An eerie moan rises up from the dark corner of the room. Sophie's eyes grow wide. She grabs my arm. We can't see anything in the shadows.

But then I see a hint of white.

"WoooooOOOOOoooooooOOOOO!"

Ghosts!

Two ghosts float toward us. Actually, it looks like they are walking, not floating, but it's hard to say since their long sheetlike bodies drag on the floor.

"WooooOOOooooooOOOOooooooOOOoooooOOO!"

Sophie clings to me and squeaks, "Don't let them eat me."

Ghosts! Sophie and I tremble together as the ghosts stare at us with eyes so black and empty they look like two ink blobs.

Sophie squeezes my arm so tightly I wince.

"We are the Minks ghosts!" moans one of the spirits. "We haunt these halls."

"WooOOOOOOO!" moans the other one.

Sophie shivers so much it's like she is outside in the snow wearing shorts. "Wh-What do you want?" She hides behind me.

I'll protect her.

Although it would be nice if Sophie considered protecting me.

"We want dinner," says the closest ghost. "You look like a tasty meal."

"WooOOOoo . . . cough, cough, ahem . . . OOOoooOO OOoooo!" says the other one. I didn't know ghosts coughed sometimes.

Something seems fishy.

"Eat her instead!" Sophie nudges me forward, toward the ghosts. "She's tastier." She nudges me harder, and I almost tip over.

"Do you have anything smaller?" asks the closest ghost. "We're looking for more of a snack."

Sophie zips open her backpack. I've never seen her move so fast. She lifts the rabbit. "Here. Eat this thing. You can have rabbit stew or something."

"Don't do that," I say. "You promised you'd give Mopey back to Anna."

"Better Mopey than us," Sophie insists. "Take it! Take it!" she says to the ghosts.

One of the ghosts bends down. At first I think the ghost has no arms, so I'm not sure how it's going to grab the rabbit, but a couple of arms pop out of its sides. They look like human arms, not ghostly arms.

Something is going on.

"This will do nicely," says the ghost. "How did you get such a tasty treat?"

"I was petting it, and it ran away," says Sophie. "It was a dumb accident. But who cares? It's yours now. Take it. Eat it. Do whatever you want."

"We will." The other ghost moans, "WooOOOoooOOO!" and the two spirits walk away with Mopey.

Then the other ghost, the one not holding the rabbit, trips.

And when the ghost tries to stand up, its entire body comes off.

Not a body.

A sheet.

It's Anna wearing a sheet.

And then Jessie takes off her sheet, too.

Sophie gasps, but the gasp only lasts a second. A look of total anger covers her face—her mouth twists into a frown, and her eyes narrow.

But then the frown changes into a smile. "I knew it was you guys the whole time."

I know she's lying, but I'm shocked at what a good liar she is. I guess I knew that about her, and I would totally believe she was telling the truth if I hadn't seen how nervous she had just been.

"I'm glad you guys are okay," I say. "I'm sorry we made you go into the basement. I'm sorry about everything."

Jessie shrugs. "I guess we're even. You hid Mopey, and we gave you a little scare."

"You didn't scare me!" insists Sophie.

"If you say so," says Jessie, rolling her eyes. Then she and Anna walk away with the rabbit.

Sophie turns to me; her smile is gone and anger once again is spread across her face.

"They had their laugh. But now it's my turn. They think we're even? No way."

"What are you going to do?" I gasp.

Sophie shrugs. "I'll think of something, don't worry."

But that's exactly what has me worried.

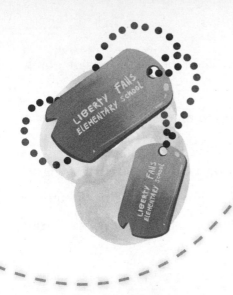

29
AARON

Some ghosts just nabbed Anna's rabbit. Well, they weren't ghosts, they were Anna and Jessie pulling a prank. But they fooled me.

And what did I do? A big fat nothing.

My dad would have done something. Someone in the army would have. Dad would be totally disappointed with me.

But I think I'm more disappointed with myself.

Then again, I have other things I should be worrying about. Brian and Seth left to snoop around and find inventions, even though we've been told over and over to touch nothing. Wesley and Norm did the same thing.

And where are Mrs. Welp, Mrs. Rosenbloom, and their entire group? Where is Principal Klein? Mr. St. Clare?

But mostly, where is Eddie?

He was my trip buddy. I should never have let him leave. I should have used my best sergeant voice and barked,

"Atten-*shun*, Private! Sit down right here. You're not going anywhere alone."

I have a lousy sergeant voice, so maybe it would have done nothing. But I didn't even try.

I take out my notebook to start my essay. If I'm going to hang here, I should get to work. These are due in the morning. I don't see other kids writing essays, but that doesn't mean I shouldn't.

I write:

Mr. Minks was a great inventor but also very weird.

No. Eddie would hate that. I erase it, and I write:

Mr. Minks was a great inventor but also very eccentric.

I don't know what to write next. My brain thinks of a million things. Maybe I should write about the secret inventions. Maybe I should write about people wandering off. Maybe I should write about Eddie's blueprint.

I slip my dad's letter out of my backpack and read the ending, the ending he always writes:

P.S. Serve. Protect. Be all you can be.

Dad wouldn't sit here reading a dumb old letter or writing an essay. He would take action. He would find Eddie. I'm not serving. Or protecting, and whatever I can be—I'm not doing that, either, even if I don't know what that is.

As I stand up, an eerie feeling crawls over me, a feeling like someone's watching, like a ghost or something.

It's Mr. Felix. He lurks in the shadows, watching us. He stands near the dining room, eyes gleaming in the dark, way scarier than a ghost. He wheezes a little, then he shuffles away.

He carries a large sack and sags a bit from its weight. Maybe it's the same sack we saw him carrying earlier. It looks bigger now, stuffed full.

Full of what?

Cleaning supplies? Bedsheets?

Or what if Jessie was right about him and Mr. St. Clare, and it's filled with stolen inventions?

I should demand he open that bag.

Instead, I look back down at my letter, wishing my dad were here, not just because I miss him, but also because he would protect us from Mr. Felix and anyone else trying to steal stuff.

P.S. Serve. Protect. Be all you can be.

I stand up. I put my letter away.

I need to make Dad proud. Earn my stripes. I'll start by finding Eddie. Teammates don't leave each other alone. That's one of the first things Dad says they learn in the army.

Teamwork.

I can serve and protect Eddie and our classmates. Maybe then I'll be all I can be.

That was the best prank ever. I bet if you ranked all-time best pranks, our ghost prank would be in the top ten, easy.

When I picture the look on Sophie's face, I break out in giggles. I didn't think that plan would work so well, not in a zillion years.

Sophie said she knew all along what we were up to. She isn't fooling me. She wouldn't fool my cats, either.

Anna and I sit with our gear, petting Mopey.

"We should put her away," I suggest. I can feel Sophie glaring at us.

Anna slips Mopey into the small cage inside her oversized backpack. "She'll go to sleep in the dark."

Across the room, a wall swings open. Well, I guess it's a door. It surprises me, because I didn't think there was a door there. I don't even see a doorknob.

For a moment, I think it might be Mr. Felix, lurking around with stolen inventions and hedge clippers.

No. It's just Brian and Seth.

"We're back!" Brian shouts. He gets down on all fours and kisses the ground.

"We didn't think we'd ever find our way here," admits Seth. "We kept finding rooms and halls. But no secret inventions."

"We found this," says Brian. He holds up a pile of broken wood and some torn seat cushions.

"What is it?" I ask.

"It was a floating sofa, or at least that's what the sign said. It was floating in the air until I sat on it, and then it stopped floating. It broke in half."

"It was really cool until we broke it," says Seth.

"Did the sign say anything on it, like *Do not sit on the sofa?*" I ask, frowning.

"Maybe," says Brian, holding up a square piece of wood that looks broken in a bunch of places. "I sort of broke the sign, too. When I fell off the sofa."

"But Brian is okay. He didn't fall far," adds Seth, patting Brian on the back. "So don't worry."

I'm not worried about Brian. I'm worried about breaking an invention. The video Mrs. Greeley played in class told us about how Minks Fantastic Floating Sofa used magnets to make the sofa hover. That way, someone could clean under the sofa without having to lift it up. The sofa was expensive, so only two or three were ever made. But the same magnets are used today in helicopters and airplanes.

So it is sort of a famous sofa.

Or, I guess, it *was* sort of a famous sofa.

I groan.

"We found other stuff, too," says Brian. "Like some bowling balls. The balls were really light. But when I tossed one across the floor, do you know what happened? It crashed through the wall."

Again, I groan. "Minks Ludicrously Light Bowling Balls were made for kids so they could throw a strike every time. The balls had ten times the power of a regular bowling ball, yet only weighed a few pounds. We learned about them in the video, remember?"

Brian shakes his head. "I slept through the video." I throw him a dirty look. "If teachers don't want us to sleep in class, they shouldn't turn off the lights when they show us stuff."

"I think the bowling ball landed in the lawn," says Seth. "It got cold in the room and snow blew inside, so we had to leave really quick."

What will Principal Klein say when he gets back? I bet

we'll all be in big, big trouble for sneaking around and ruining stuff. I doubt detention will be a big enough punishment for destroying famous inventions.

Wesley and Norm walk in from the entryway. I'm glad kids are finding their way back, and I'm sure they were way more careful than Brian and Seth.

"We found musical instruments," says Norm.

"There was an entire closet filled with them. Enough for an entire band." Wesley holds up a banjo. "This banjo plays itself."

"Let's hear it," I call out.

Wesley frowns. "I mean, it used to play itself. It broke when I dropped it down the staircase."

Or maybe they weren't way more careful than Brian and Seth.

If this house survives the fifth-grade class of Liberty Falls Elementary, it will be a miracle.

It's bad enough that Mr. St. Clare and Mr. Felix are stealing inventions. But if we destroy all the inventions they don't swipe, there won't be any left at all.

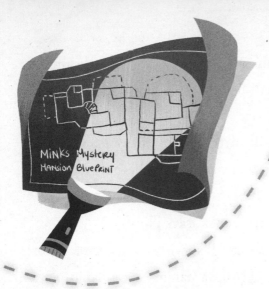

31

EDDIE

I zigzag down this weird hall. There are no doors. Only a few lights. I have no idea if I'm in the front of the house, the back of the house, or what. I'm not even sure what floor I'm on. The hall seems to rise up, but then it feels like it slides down.

I remember a poem my great-great-great-grandfather wrote.

Sometimes you must zag,
Sometimes you must zig,
But to get anywhere
You must always think big.

Maybe that's a clue to the hidden inventions. Or maybe it's just a poem that has nothing to do with anything.

I pass doors. Some have paintings of beds, and some have paintings of toilets. I don't go in those rooms.

Finally, after way too much zigging and way too much

zagging, there's a large painting of two huge eyeballs up ahead. It's a little scary, actually. It's like the picture stares at me. But it's a door to somewhere.

I push it open.

I'm in a room that has a large round table in the middle with a dozen chairs. There are colorful beads hanging from the ceiling, and I brush them away to walk inside. When I hit the light switch, the room is cast in a pale reddish glow.

This must be the séance room. Lady Minks often held séances to talk to ghosts, mostly to tell them to stop haunting her.

I'm pretty sure she never actually talked to any, or at least I've never heard of any talking back.

But maybe I can talk to my great-great-great-grandfather. Maybe he can tell me where the secret inventions are, and maybe he can help me stop Mr. St. Clare and Mr. Felix.

I don't know how this works. I sit on a chair. Part of me is sort of scared to be calling for ghosts, but I need to get back and save the house, and I can't do it alone or if I'm lost.

"Um, hello, ghosts?" I ask.

There is no response.

"I'm not sure if you're listening, but if Mr. Minks is here, then I could use some help. I'm your great-great-great-grandson. So, hello."

Again, there is no answer.

I'm glad there's no answer, and I'm not glad at the same time.

"I'm sort of lost in the house, and there's a plan to steal stuff," I say. "So, all you need to do is help me get back. I mean, I'd love to find those secret inventions, too. You want me to have them, right? That's why you left the blueprint? But if you help me get back, I'll help protect the house, too. Does that sound like a good deal? I'm just lost and need to get back to Aaron."

I think I hear a soft breeze. Maybe not. No. There's nothing.

"So, maybe you could just point the way or send some help?"

Again, nothing. If a ghost appeared, I'd probably scream, so it's probably better that none came. But I'm desperate.

"Never mind, then," I say, and stand up.

I push open the door to the room and step out.

OOMPH!

I bump right into Aaron.

"Hey!" he yelps.

I step off his foot. "What are you doing here?"

"Looking for you. I thought you might be lost."

"I would never get lost." I cross my arms and roll my eyes. "I am a Minks and we never get lost." I lift my nose. "I certainly don't need help from you."

"Oh, okay," says Aaron. He looks down at his feet.

Why do I do that? I take a deep breath. "Sorry. Maybe I'm a little lost. Thanks for looking for me."

Aaron lifts his head up. "That's what friends do for each other, right? We're a team."

"We're a team," I agree. But I also think, *And we're friends? I hope so.*

My great-great-great-grandfather once wrote this poem, too:

Sometimes you must zig,
Sometimes you must zag,
But working with others
Is sometimes a drag.

My great-great-great-grandfather was brilliant, but he didn't know everything.

"How did you find me?" I ask.

Aaron shrugs. "I don't know. I was going another way, and then I just had a feeling you might be down this hall."

"Did a ghost show you the way?"

Aaron looks at me as if I'm bonkers. "Of course not. Why?"

"Never mind."

"Did you find any secret inventions?"

"I'm a Minks. Of course I did." But then I swallow the words. I look at Aaron, frowning at me. "No. Nothing."

I tell Aaron everything I know. I tell him about the room with the maps and the big dollar numbers and the holes, and how I'm positive Mr. St. Clare and Mr. Felix are stealing things. I tell him how I'm convinced they are looking for the secret inventions, but I'm confident they haven't found them yet.

But they are getting closer.

Aaron nods. "At least with all this snow, I don't think they can get away. You heard Principal Klein. All the roads are closed. Those stolen inventions are probably trapped here, too."

"The blizzard won't last forever. I'll have to think of a plan to stop them."

"We'll think of a plan together."

"I'm a Minks and I . . ." I stop talking when I see Aaron's frown grow. I shake my head. "Of course. That's a good idea. We'll think of something together. First, do you know the way back?"

Aaron points toward a door. "There's a winding stairway down there, behind the painting of that winding stairway. It'll take us to the front hall."

A few moments later, we enter the ballroom. Some kids look up, but most don't give us a second glance. People ignore me all the time. I'm used to it.

Once I get back to my pillow and blanket, I unfold my

blueprint. It still may offer some clues. If we can find the secret inventions before Mr. St. Clare and Mr. Felix do, we can protect them.

We need to find them tonight. Tonight will be our only chance.

I can save my family's house and my family's legacy. Our history and maybe even our fortune.

But it feels like a waste of time. The blueprint reveals nothing new.

Aaron looks over my shoulder. "Why couldn't he just write, *Secret inventions, look here?* What's the point of inventing things and never sharing them with anyone?"

"I think the inventions were so great he wanted to keep them away from people who made no sense, or people who might steal them like Mr. St. Clare and Mr. Felix. Maybe he figured anyone clever enough to find them would be clever enough to know what to do with them."

"To share them with the world."

"So the entire world can profit."

We stare at the blueprint, but I've stared at it a zillion times, and I don't see anything that shows where a secret invention room might be hidden.

"We should ask the other kids for help," Aaron suggests.

"No."

"Why not?"

"Just because."

Sure, Aaron can help. We're a team. But Brian and Seth and some of the people in my class would rather create trouble than stop it. My dad always says a Minks needs no one. He might not be completely right. But not everyone makes as much sense as Aaron and me.

"Have you tried putting heat against it?" Aaron asks, pointing to the map.

I blink. "What do you mean?"

"Some invisible ink can only be seen with heat," says Aaron. "When I was a kid, my dad used to leave secret messages for me, usually jokes and stuff, but he wrote them with invisible ink. Here's a good one: What did the army private say to the armored forces unit after they saved his life?"

"What?"

"Tanks a lot!" I don't smile, because it's not really funny. "The armored forces unit uses tanks in war," explains Aaron. "I guess it's only funny if you know that."

"I guess so."

"Anyway, maybe Minks wrote secret messages with invisible ink. We just need something hot to read them. I think I have something we can use." Aaron fishes in his backpack. He lifts a small, thin flashlight. "This is my dad's. I keep it with me sometimes. It reminds me of him." He flicks the switch on and puts it under the blueprint. "Give it a minute to heat up."

The blueprint is old and brittle. I'm afraid the heat might damage the paper, and then I won't even have a secret antique blueprint to help me find secret inventions, if there are any secret inventions. But then the blueprint changes. At first, I think the light is burning the blueprint, and I yelp and am about to shout at Aaron to turn off the flashlight now!

But I'm wrong about the damage. Instead, a line appears, a blue line that was not on the map before. It leads from the grand ballroom, up the grand staircase, around a hall and then stops.

"A secret trail," Aaron whispers.

"But to where?"

Some letters fade up next to a door on the second floor. I recognize Minks's handwriting. It reads:

To find this clue you must be bright.

With a little twist you'll see the light.

Right next to it are two numbers.

0-1.

Aaron turns off the flashlight, and all the lines and words disappear. We stare at each other. Before I know what I'm doing, I'm racing Aaron up the grand staircase.

32
CHLOE

Sophie is in a bad mood. It seems like she's always in a bad mood lately, but her mood now is worse than usual. She keeps mumbling about getting even. I wish she would stop thinking about it.

I can't stop feeling terrible for helping her hide Mopey in the first place. I feel horrible for letting her send Jessie and Anna to the basement. I could have said something. I didn't, and saying nothing is just as bad as doing something bad.

My mom says that what we think deep down inside isn't as important as what we do. She says if you're all nice inside, but you act mean, then you're not nice at all. She says actions speak louder than words.

So maybe I'm not nice at all.

I notice Sophie isn't glaring at Anna and Jessie anymore,

or mumbling about revenge. That's a relief. Instead, she's looking at the entryway. She points as Eddie and Aaron run toward it. "Where do you think they're going?"

"Exploring? I wish everyone would just stay here."

"Why?"

"Because we were told to stay here. And kids are breaking things."

"We should follow those guys."

"What are you talking about?"

"Think about it. If anyone knows where those secret inventions are hidden, it's Eddie, right? He is the great-great-whatever of this dumb Minks guy. He says he's been to this house a zillion times. I've been watching him. I think he has a map or something. He's been acting strange. I know he's always strange, but he's been acting even stranger."

"He's not strange," I say.

"Yes he is."

"Okay, a little strange," I say, not wanting to argue. "But that's not always bad."

"Yes, it's always bad. But we need to follow them. If they're off to find something, I want to know what. If they know where secret inventions are hidden, I want some."

"I don't think we're allowed to keep any inventions," I say. "They're supposed to help the world, remember?"

"Sometimes, I just don't get you." Sophie rolls her eyes and shakes her head. "Come on." She springs up and moves toward the staircase. "Let's go."

I think about staying behind. I don't want to be involved in her plans anymore.

But I don't. I hurry after her. That's the sort of thing best friends do, even if I wonder why we're still friends at all.

As soon as we get to the entryway, we see Eddie and Aaron hurrying up the final steps of the grand stairway. We climb after them, turning left at the top like they did.

I want to tell Sophie we should go back. We could get in big trouble. It might not be safe. But Sophie doesn't slow down, so I follow.

We peek around the corner. A door is closing up ahead of us. Just before it does, I see the heel of a sneaker.

We creep toward the door as quietly as we can. I don't know what's in the room. If there are secret inventions, then I hope they are funtastic. Maybe if we find something, Sophie will change her mind. Maybe she will agree all inventions should "profit the world," just like Mr. Minks wanted.

She changed her mind about stealing Mopey, until she changed her mind and stole Mopey. So maybe she'll change her mind about this, too.

There is no painting on this door. It's just a door. But one more thing strikes me as strange. I point to the doorknob.

There's a small button lock on it. "Aren't those sorts of locks inside doors, not outside them?"

Maybe there are ghosts inside, and Lady Minks needed to lock them in?

I decide not to mention that. I know how scared Sophie is of ghosts.

Besides, she's already twisting the knob and opening the door.

The door creaks. We peer inside. I'm ready to jump back and away from flying ghosts.

But there's nothing to frighten us. It's a closet, and it looks empty. No ghost swirl around, but there's no Eddie or Aaron, either.

It's like they disappeared.

"Is this a joke?" Sophie asks, putting her hands on her hips, frowning.

"Maybe they didn't go in here?" I'm just as confused as Sophie.

"Of course they went in here." She pauses. "Maybe they fell down a hole."

The room is dark, but a string hangs from a lightbulb on the ceiling. She pulls the string, but the light doesn't turn on. Sophie shakes her head. "What's with lights and this house? The basement light doesn't work. This light doesn't work. You'd think a great inventor could at least get his dumb lights working."

I remember the basement stairwell and shiver a little.

Sophie taps her foot on the floor, frowning. She gets down and rubs her hand along it. Then she stands up and throws her arms in the air. "I don't know. It's just a closet. We must have been seeing things. We must be delirious from skipping dinner."

"You ate granola bars," I say, crinkling my nose.

"But only one or two. That's hardly enough for a balanced meal." I continue to stare at her. "You're not still mad about that, are you? I told you I'd give you one later."

"But only if I wrote a report for you," I remind her, my hands on my hips.

"Sounds fair to me. Anyway, let's go downstairs."

"Fine." We turn around, but I'm hungry and annoyed at Sophie. Still, we should go back to the ballroom before we get in trouble for wandering around, or get lost in this house.

I hope Eddie and Aaron are fine. I shouldn't worry. Eddie comes here all the time. He wouldn't get lost.

Sophie stomps away, and I follow.

Mom always says that a gray day is just a blue day waiting to happen. I just wish the blue sky would come out already, because this entire day and night have been really, really gray. And I'm not only talking about the snow clouds outside.

When we get downstairs, instead of walking over to our pillows, Sophie heads straight to Anna and Jessie.

"What are you doing?" I ask.

Sophie looks down at her pants. "There is no way this stain is ever coming out. It's time to get even."

I don't know what to say. "But . . . but . . ."

"What's your problem now?"

"It's just that, well, getting even isn't nice."

"You know what's wrong with you? You want to be nice all the time. Being nice all the time is dumb."

"You used to be nice." My voice cracks. Sophie's eyes narrow and she stabs her finger at me. She looks very . . . un nice.

Before I can say anything else, Sophie marches straight to Anna and Jessie. I follow her, a step behind. My stomach growls, and it's not just because I'm hungry. I already feel guilty for so many things I've done or haven't done. This trip is not turning out to be funtastic at all.

When we get to Jessie and Anna, Sophie frowns. She bows her head. "I haven't been very nice." I step back, my mouth open. Maybe I'm wrong about Sophie.

Anna and Jessie look up. They look as surprised as I do.

Sophie continues looking down at them. "I'd like to make it up to you."

Jessie doesn't say anything, but Anna manages to squeak out, "That's okay."

Sophie shakes her head. "I want to apologize."

"Great," says Anna. She waits. I wait. Jessie waits.

"But not here," says Sophie. "I want to show you something first."

"What do you want to show her?" asks Jessie. She eyes Sophie like she doesn't trust her, but Sophie seems sincere. I'm glad she changed her mind about doing something mean to Anna. Maybe the nicer Sophie is back again.

"You have to see it," says Sophie.

I wonder what it is.

Jessie stands up. "Whatever you want to show to Anna, you can show to me."

Sophie shrugs. "Fine, you can come, too."

"I will," says Jessie.

I'm proud of Sophie, and I feel bad for thinking badly of her.

Jessie and Anna stand up. Sophie waves them toward her. "It's upstairs."

What does she want to show them? We were just upstairs and didn't see anything interesting at all. We go to the entryway and head up the grand staircase. "What's up here?" I whisper to Sophie.

Sophie just shakes her head. I guess it will be a surprise for me, too.

"Where are we going?" Jessie asks as we reach the top of the stairwell.

"It's around the corner," says Sophie.

I'm confused, but Sophie sounds like she really feels bad. We turn the corner and Sophie opens the closet we looked at just a few minutes ago. "In here."

"What's in here?" asks Jessie, peering in. "It's an empty closet."

"Walk in and I'll show you," says Sophie.

I don't see anything in there, but I didn't go into the closet. What did Sophie find? And why didn't she show me before we went back downstairs?

I'm starting to get a bad feeling about this.

Jessie and Anna walk into the closet, but Sophie doesn't go in. There isn't enough room for three people anyway. Instead, she shuts the door and presses the button on the doorknob, locking them inside.

"Hey!" Jessie shouts from inside the closet, although her voice is muffled. One of them, Jessie or Anna, bangs on the door.

Sophie grabs my hand and leads me away.

"You're not going to leave them in there, are you?" I ask.

"Of course. What did you think I was going to do?"

"Apologize?"

"You're funny. I never apologize. You should know that."

I guess I do know that. I should have known that.

I want to run back and open the door. Locking them in a

closet is just cruel. I can still hear banging as we turn the corner. "They're probably scared," I say.

"That's the idea."

I walk down the stairs with Sophie, wondering if I should turn around and let them out.

As soon as I can sneak away, I'll run back upstairs and let them out.

I slow down. No, I should turn around right now. I shouldn't have to sneak to do the right thing. Sneaking around and keeping quiet just makes me as mean as Sophie.

"Why are you going so slow? You're not thinking of doing anything dumb, are you? Like letting them out?" Sophie asks, glaring at me. "Promise you won't."

"Promise?"

"Yeah. Best Friends' Honor."

I didn't even know Best Friends' Honor was something to promise on.

"I don't want to promise."

"You have to," Sophie says.

"Why?"

"Because we're the awesome twosome, right?"

"You mean the terrific twosome."

"Whatever."

We still are?

I take a big gulp. "Fine. I promise. Best Friends' Honor." It sounds like a real binding promise, too.

I just made the worst promise in the world. I need to stand up for myself, and that means standing up for being nice.

But I promised, Best Friends' Honor and everything. And I can't break that, even though I didn't know that was a *thing*. Breaking your word is mean.

All I want to do is the nice thing. So why do I feel like I keep doing the opposite?

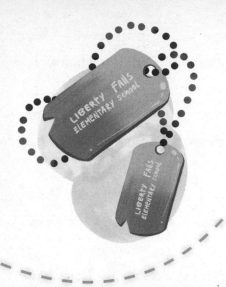

33

AARON

We're in a bizarro room. Lots of rooms in this house are crazy, but this one might be the craziest of them all.

Everything is upside down.

We entered the closet, and then Eddie and I were clueless. Except we weren't. We had a clue. *To find this clue you must be bright. With a little twist you'll see the light.* That gave me an idea to twist the lightbulb. A secret panel slid out and we climbed through.

Then we stepped into this secret and crazy upside-down room.

We stand on the ceiling. The only other thing on the ground is a small black garbage can in the corner. Everything else is above us. There is a leather couch and a comfy chair hanging from the ceiling. There is a dresser and a coffee table with books and folders and pens, all upside down. There's even a magazine, and a list of chores that I can barely read. The paper says *Chores* but it only lists one: *Go out the trash.*

I guess it means, *Take out the trash.* I've got my own list of chores I do at home, like mowing the lawn and shoveling snow.

When I get home, I'll be shoveling snow.

Is all that stuff hanging over us glued down? It must be. It must have taken a whole lot of work to paste all that stuff into place. I don't have any idea why anyone would bother. I jump up, but it is a really high ceiling. We couldn't reach that stuff, even if we stood on each other's shoulders.

I'm not sure why we would want to reach any of that stuff, anyway. It's all normal stuff, just upside down.

The room's also got a large clock on the wall. That's upside down, too. I have to turn my head around to read it.

Wow. It's late, way-past-my-bedtime late. Now that I know the time, I yawn. I didn't realize how tired I was getting.

"Why would anyone build a room upside down?" I ask. "I mean, that's just bonkers. What would you use it for? You could use a ladder to reach the couch maybe, but then you'd just fall right off and crash on the floor. Or fall onto the ceiling, I guess."

"It is strange," he admits. "My great-great-great-grandfather was brilliant, but he was also a weirdo."

"He was eccentric," I say.

Eddie shakes his head. "That's just another word for weirdo."

I shrug.

Still, there must be some reason why an upside-down room is in the house, and there must be some reason it can only be reached by a hidden door in a closet. I just have no idea what those reasons could be.

The floor below me looks dusty. You can see our footprints. No one has been in this room since forever. Maybe not since Mr. Minks was alive.

No one might even know this room is here, except us.

And if no one knows about this room, then this could be the room with the hidden inventions. Or not. It seems one puzzle just leads to another puzzle.

But then an idea grabs me.

"Remember what Mr. St. Clare said?"

"About what?" asks Eddie. "He said lots of stuff."

"About how Mr. Minks wanted to create inventions that turned the world upside down? Mr. St. Clare said it when we first got here. He also said the Mr. Minks invented the upside-down cake."

"Don't talk about that thief Mr. St. Clare," says Eddie. "Or about cake. My stomach is growling enough after skipping dinner."

My stomach rumbles, agreeing with his stomach. "Sorry. But now we're in an upside-down room. That can't just be coincidence, right? Minks wanted to make us see things differently. Surprise us." I look around the room. "Maybe we're just not looking at this room the right way."

"How about if I do this?" Eddie bends down so he looks at the room upside down, through his legs. His face starts turning red as blood rushes to it. "Maybe now I'm seeing things the right way?"

"What do you see?"

"Um, an upside-down room that's not upside down? It just looks like a regular room now. And my head hurts."

He straightens himself up.

"So that didn't work?"

"It worked if the plan was to give myself a headache."

I take a deep breath. There has to be something we're missing. Something epic. Maybe even something *hidden invention* epic.

"Look at that." Eddie points to a mirror hanging on the wall just above us. But in the mirror, the room looks right side up.

"Cool." Most mirrors reflect things backward, but this one reflects things upside down.

"Maybe that's why he built the room," Eddie suggests. "To test an upside-down mirror."

"Why would anyone need an upside-down mirror?"

"To see things if you built an upside-down room, obviously."

"Wouldn't it just be, I don't know, easier to build rooms that aren't upside down?"

Eddie nods. "Sure, but who knows what my great-great-great-grandfather was thinking about anything."

"Yeah, but it's still a pretty freaky invention." And then I think about it a little more. "And you know what? Maybe it's a secret invention."

Eddie raises his eyebrow. "You might be right. I've never heard of him building an upside-down mirror. And where there's one secret invention . . ."

He doesn't have to finish the sentence.

But where are they? I don't see anything hidden—unless the furniture and things aren't glued and bolted, but are floating. Maybe he invented a floating room?

I don't think so. Still, building an entire room just to test a mirror seems like wasted time. And I don't think an upside-down mirror is worth a fortune, either.

I walk over to the panel where we entered. It shut itself after we crawled through. I can't get it to budge. I pry it with my fingernails, but it seems locked in place. I use all my strength, but I don't have army-sergeant strength, just me strength.

And I don't think anyone could move it, anyway.

"I have some bad news," I say to Eddie as I pry and pull. "I think we're trapped in here."

34
JESSIE

"Let us out!" I cry, banging on the closet door.

Sophie's laughing fades as her and Chloe's footsteps grow farther and farther away.

I bump against Anna. It's dark in the closet. The only light comes from a crack at the bottom of the door. It's cramped in here, too. There is barely enough room for Anna and me to stand.

A dark closet is almost as scary as a dark basement stairway. I remind myself to be as brave as my cats.

"Maybe there's a light?" Anna asks.

"Good idea."

I reach out my hands. I think I saw a string dangling in front of us right before the door closed. Maybe it's connected to a light bulb. My hand hits the string, but then I have to wave my hand around before I finally grab it. I give the string a tug. It clicks.

Nothing else happens.

"I guess the light's broken or something," I say. "Figures."

I'm facing Anna, and she's facing me, which is just sort of awkward because we breathe on each other.

"I hate the dark," she says, banging on the door.

"No one is going to hear us," I say.

"We could be trapped here forever," says Anna. Fear rises in her voice. "And who will feed Mopey? She'll be scared without me."

I need to think, but it's hard to think with someone breathing on you and when everything is so dark. Mama drinks a lot of green tea, and she says green tea helps your eyesight. I should start drinking a lot of green tea. It might help me see in dark closets. "Maybe the bulb needs to be twisted tighter. They come loose. Can you help me up?"

I can't see anything in the darkness, but Anna grabs my foot, and I step into her hands.

I reach around for a lightbulb, and when I feel it, I give it a small twist.

The light doesn't turn on, but something else happens.

There's a CRRREAKKKK.

And a small door in the back of the closet slides open. Light streams in from another room.

"Should we go in?" Anna asks.

"Of course," I say, like it's nothing, but it's not nothing. Who knows what's on the other side of that door? I take a deep breath and crawl through the opening. Anna crawls in behind me, and then suddenly we're upside down.

Well, not upside down, but we're standing on a ceiling, a ceiling that is actually a floor, and above us is a floor that's actually the ceiling.

That's not the only surprising thing—Eddie and Aaron are here, too. They sit right in the middle of the room.

"Grab that panel!" yells Aaron, pointing behind us. "Behind you . . ."

There's a click, and when I turn, I see the little door we crawled through has slid back into place.

"Never mind," Aaron says with a loud sigh.

"Wait. How did you guys get in here?" I ask.

"Through the panel, same as you," says Aaron. "*To find this clue you must be bright. With a little twist you'll see the light.* You didn't have the clue?"

"I don't know what you're talking about," I say.

"Well, clue or not, we're stuck here," says Eddie, crossing his arms. "That door was the only way out. We found a secret invention, though. Not that it will do us any good." He points to a mirror.

The mirror looks like an ordinary mirror, but then I realize it's not an ordinary mirror. Everything reflects upside down, which makes the room look right side up.

"That's pretty awesome," I say, peering closer at it. It's

weird to see my face upside down. I frown and it looks like a smile. "At least that's one invention Mr. St. Clare and Mr. Felix didn't steal. I know you guys don't believe me but—"

Eddie interrupts. "We believe you."

"We have proof they are stealing things, too," adds Aaron.

"Where? What? How?" I stand straight, like Patches does when she's surprised. She usually pricks her ears up, too, but I can't do that.

"I found a room with all sorts of notes and maps," says Eddie. "Those thieves have it all figured out. But I don't think they've found secret inventions. Not yet anyway. And I don't think they know about this room."

"If my cats were here, they would stop them," I say.

"I'm not sure your cats would scare Mr. Felix," says Eddie.

"That's because he hasn't met my cats."

As I join Eddie and Aaron on the floor, Anna wraps her arms around herself and rocks in place. I force a smile. "Don't worry, Anna. I'm sure we'll be fine and so will Mopey. There has to be a way out, right? No one would build a room with no way out."

"My great-great-great-grandfather was a little unusual," says Eddie. "So who knows?"

"He was eccentric," says Aaron. Eddie shrugs, and Aaron yawns. "Sorry. It's been a long day."

Yawns are contagious, like the chicken pox. I yawn, and so do Anna and Eddie. I'd love to put my head on a pillow. If I could float, I'd sleep on the sofa glued to the floor above me.

Above me.

There's a window, but it's too high to reach, and I don't see a door, either. It's weird that all those magazines are glued on the coffee table, and Minks wrote a list of chores and pasted that down, too. The room reminds me of a fun house.

I stare at the list of chores. Well, it's not a list. There's only one thing on it: *Go out the trash.*

"Strange," says Anna, looking at the note. "My dad always says that I have to *take* out the trash, not *go* out the trash."

"We thought the same thing," says Eddie. "But it was written a long time ago. Maybe that's what they used to say back then."

"And why is there a garbage can on the floor?" Anna speaks so softly her words just sort of disappear into the air. She points to the plain black trash can pushed against the wall. We have one just like it in our kitchen at home.

"To throw things away?" suggests Aaron.

"But it's the only thing that's not upside down in the entire room," Anna says.

She walks over to the trash can and kicks it. It doesn't move.

Anna smiles and then jumps inside.

And disappears.

"Anna? Where are you? What happened?" I gasp.

I run over to the trash can. Eddie and Aaron dash right behind me.

That's when I see it's not a trash can. It's a hole! *Go out the trash* was a clue about how to get out of here. I don't know where the hole leads, but at least it goes somewhere that's not here.

I hop in, too.

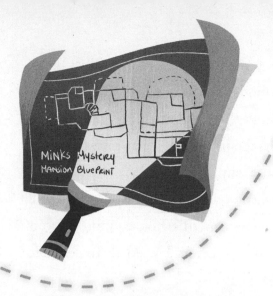

35

EDDIE

I land on top of Jessie, who landed on top of Anna, and then Aaron lands on top of me. We spill out into the front hall. I end up under the coatrack an inch away. One of its arms reaches out . . .

TWANG!

. . . and just misses my head before it snaps back into position.

I rub my shoulder where Aaron accidentally kicked me. Jessie rubs her head where I accidentally kicked her. Anna rubs a dozen places where we all accidentally kicked her.

"Everyone okay?" asks Aaron.

We all moan, but I think we're fine, mostly.

"At least we're out of the room," Jessie says. "I would have landed on my feet if I were a cat."

"That was smart thinking, Anna," I say. "I guess that list of chores made sense after all."

Jessie and Anna hurry off to the ballroom. They must want to check on Anna's rabbit. We follow behind.

Not many people know this, but my great-great-great-grandfather had a phobia about rabbits. That means he was scared of them. I'm not sure why.

He may have been a little odd, but he was also brilliant. There has to be more secrets in this house, more secrets that are waiting to be found—secrets I need to find before Mr. St. Clare and Mr. Felix do.

Secrets that can save my family and our house.

Secrets that can "profit the world."

But it's so late! I rub my eyes. There are only a few lights on in the ballroom, so it's mostly dark in here. Some kids breathe heavily. They're already asleep.

I slip under my blanket. I wish I had a toothbrush and pajamas, and this hard floor hurts to lay on, but I'm so, so tired.

Still, my mind doesn't quite want to sleep. It keeps filling with thoughts of secret inventions and criminals hatching schemes. I think of riches, and my family, and my weirdo great-great-great-grandfather.

I picture Mr. Felix writing in his journal: *Take everything.*

Meanwhile, I lay here under a blanket.

I sit up. I unfold my blueprint. There must be something here. Something I'm not seeing. It's hard to see the blueprint in the dark, but I squint to make out the details.

"You're looking at your blueprint, aren't you?" asks Aaron. He's lying down, wrapped in his blanket with his eyes closed.

"How do you know?"

"I could hear the paper rustling." Aaron opens his eyes and sits up, too. I'm glad he does. "Maybe we should try to put heat on it again? That worked last time. And then can we sleep? We can look again in the morning."

I nod my head. "Sure."

"I'll grab my flashlight." Aaron sits up and reaches into his backpack. Soon, his flashlight is shining under the blueprint.

We stare at the paper. After a few seconds, more lines form. More secret paths are revealed. I hold my breath.

There is a lot more on this map than we noticed earlier.

"What's that?" asks Sophie. She stands directly over us, glaring down.

"It's nothing," I say. Aaron shuts off the flashlight. The lines on the blueprint fade.

"That's not a nothing," says Sophie, staring at us. Her mouth is puckered in a thoughtful frown. "You've been look-ing at something all day, something secret. And I want to know what it is." She points down at the paper I'm holding. "Is that a map of this house?"

"Of course not," I say, looking away and biting my lip.

I'm not about to share this with someone like Sophie.

"You're a bad liar. Unlike me." She smiles. This is not her

I'm nice and fooling teachers smile, but the smile I've seen from her when someone trips in the hallway. It's an unfriendly smile. She bends down to grab the blueprint. "Let me see that."

"No."

She tugs at the paper, but I don't let go.

"Give that to me." She pulls the edges.

"Be careful. You'll rip it!"

With a forceful tug, she tears off a corner.

ZZZZZTTT!

She stumbles back, holding the corner. My hands start shaking, but at least she didn't damage the blueprint too much. Sophie steps over and reaches down again. "I said, give me that!" She wraps her hands around the paper, wrinkling and crumbling it beneath her hands.

"Watch it! You're ruining it!" I cry.

"I. Want. It. Now." Sophie yanks the paper away.

RRRIPP!!!

The paper is so old and brittle it doesn't just rip in half, but the half that Sophie holds dissolves into dozens of small pieces. The half still in my hand begins to flake into small shards.

"L-Look what you've done," I say, my voice shaking.

"That's what you get for not sharing," says Sophie.

She stomps away, without even an apology.

I open my mouth, but nothing comes out. There were more hidden lines. There might have been a secret. We might have found inventions.

Instead, I have nothing but paper dust scattered on the floor around me.

"We could try to tape everything back together," says Aaron.

But we both know there are too many pieces to try that.

"We don't know if there even are hidden inventions, not for sure, right?" asks Aaron.

"I know."

But there were messages! Clues! And now I have nothing.

If anyone finds secret inventions, it will be Mr. St. Clare and Mr. Felix. It won't be me.

My family's legacy is left in the hands of two thieves.

I throw my head down on the pillow. A few kids snore lightly. Some of them toss and turn, but the room is mostly quiet. Even Sophie snuggles into her blanket next to the already-sleeping Chloe.

I think of my parents. I think of all my plans. My eyes water and I sniffle.

"We can still look around in the morning," says Aaron.

"What's the point?"

"We can still stop the robbery. We just need to get everyone together . . ."

"Leave me alone."

"But . . ."

"Stop it!"

I bury my head under the blanket. I shouldn't have snapped at Aaron. And he's right. We can still stop the thieves from stealing everything. But it's not his family's future that is lying in pieces on the floor.

Eventually, I hear Aaron's steady breathing. I might be the only one in the ballroom still awake.

Even with my eyes closed, all I can see are broken inventions, stolen inventions, and my family losing our house.

I might never fall asleep again.

36

CHLOE

I'm one of the first to wake the next morning. I've always been an early riser. Mom says if I were a bird, I'd catch the early worm. Do late-sleeping birds go hungry? That would be a shame. Some birds can't help sleeping late.

Maybe I should start collecting worms in the morning and leave them for birds.

I step over Sophie, who is sleeping with her mouth wide open, and I look out the window.

Wow. I'm not collecting worms today.

It stopped snowing, but the snow covers half the window. It must be four feet deep. I have never seen this much snow, not even in pictures. We could be trapped here for days!

There's one more thing I realize, too— none of the missing kids or adults ever came back last night. Neither did Principal Klein or Mr. St. Clare. Half the pillows and blankets in the ballroom are still unused, piled in the corner.

What if they're not fine? What if something happened to everyone? I bite my lip. We should do something!

No. I shake my head. I'm being silly. Teachers and principals are way too smart to let something bad happen to them.

They might not have had a soft pillow or blanket like I have, though. I should feel very lucky that I got to sleep in the mansion. I hope everyone in this room appreciates how lucky they are, too.

"We'll be trapped forever!" yells Brian. His yell surprises me, and I jump. I didn't expect him to be an early riser. He also wakes everyone up. "Help! Help! This is horrible!" He points to the window.

I guess he doesn't appreciate how lucky we are.

"What's going on?" asks a yawning Sophie, stirring. She sits up. Her braided hair, swooping around her head, is still perfectly in place. My hair usually looks all messy in the morning. I don't even like to look in the mirror when I wake up.

"There's forty feet of snow outside!" hollers Seth. "We'll starve!"

Jessie walks over to the window. "There's a lot of snow, but it'll melt. Eventually."

Jessie's back! Maybe Sophie opened the closet door for them.

I lean over to Sophie. "That was super nice of you to let Jessie and Anna out of the closet," I say.

"I didn't let them out," she grumbles. "Maybe the lock was broken."

I nod and don't say anything. I didn't help them, either. I made a promise to Sophie, but that just makes me as mean as her.

"I brought a bag of chips," says Norm. "We could all eat maybe one chip apiece? Did anyone else bring food?"

As soon as Norm mentions food, I remember how hungry I am. I didn't eat much for dinner other than a piece of bread and a small spoonful of horrible oatmeal.

A few kids raise their hands. They have food. We can eat!

But between them we have two bags of potato chips and two bananas. That's not going to be enough for breakfast for all of us.

I look at Sophie and her backpack next to her. It's open a crack. There must be twenty granola bars inside, or more. I jump up, point to her bag, and say, "Sophie has . . ." but then Sophie fixes me a look that says *Don't you dare say anything*, and I swallow my words.

"Sophie has what?" asks Aaron.

"Sophie has a big appetite. That's all," I say quietly.

"Well, we all need to share what we have equally," says Aaron.

"Of course," I answer, looking down and feeling silly.

Sophie whispers to me, "It's a secret. Best Friends' Honor."

"But everyone is hungry." We should be sharing. I should say something.

I know Sophie thinks that I say *I'm sorry* too much. I know she says I'm too nice to people.

But why are those bad things?

"Don't worry, we have food," says Jessie. I didn't see her leave the room. She and Anna walk in with a tall pile of cardboard boxes: *Instant Scrambled Egg Breakfast with Blueberry Muffin Cardboard Dessert.*

"They're empty," says Jessie. "But they are made of edible blueberry muffin cardboard. The boxes taste sort of like gym socks. But we won't starve."

"We're supposed to eat cardboard?" whines Seth. He doesn't look happy about it. Most kids don't look too happy about it.

"Would you rather eat one-hundred-and-fifty-year-old pickles?" asks Jessie. "We found a jar of those, too."

"Never mind. Cardboard sounds good," says Seth.

Sophie whispers to me. "We could eat stewed rabbit for breakfast."

I'm not sure if she's kidding.

Aaron looks at the boxes and counts them. "Each of us can have a box. That's not so bad."

Next to me, Sophie peels open one of her granola bars and takes a bite from it. She slinks down so people can't see her.

The bar looks delicious. I bet I could just grab one and she wouldn't stop me. But then I'd be selfish, and being selfish is mean. I stand up, and when I do, I kick over her backpack.

"Whoops!" I exclaim. "Look what I did!"

Granola bars spill across the floor.

"It was an accident," I say. I feel a little guilty about lying, but I don't feel very guilty about lying. I've never been good at it, and now I also feel bad about suddenly being pretty good at it.

Everyone looks at us.

"What's that?" Norm asks.

Sophie looks up, startled. "Nothing."

Jessie and Norm strut over to us. Sophie tries to scoop up her granola bars and stuff them into her backpack, but she's too slow.

"Hey! You've got an entire backpack of granola bars," says Norm.

Sophie lifts her chin up. "I was just about to tell everyone." But I don't believe her. I don't know if I can believe anything she says. "I found them in the front hallway."

"How many do you have?" asks Norm.

"A lot," admits Sophie.

"We can all have maybe half a granola bar along with a cardboard box," says Aaron, quickly counting the bars on the floor. "We should be fine, at least until lunch."

"I don't see why I should have to eat a box," says Sophie, "when I found the granola bars."

"Maybe we should fight for it." Jessie stretches her hands out like cat claws and she hisses.

Sophie bares her teeth. "You don't frighten me."

I don't like this one bit. We shouldn't fight. Fighting is never a good idea, and especially not now, when we are all trapped in a house together. "How about if we have a snowball fight instead?" I suggest. "That's sort of like a fight."

Jessie lowers her claws and nods. "Fine with me." She seems relieved.

"Whatever," Sophie says.

"Simple rules," I say. "We'll have two teams. If a snowball hits you, you're out."

"And the last team standing wins all the granola bars," says Jessie. "The losers eat cardboard." She turns around. "Who wants to be on my team?"

I think she expects most of us to join her, but then Sophie stands up. "If you join my team, you not only get a granola bar, but I'll invite you to my next birthday party."

"I wouldn't even want to go to your dumb birthday party," says Jessie.

Sophie shrugs. "I wouldn't let you come anyway."

But most kids don't feel the same way Jessie feels. Everyone wants to go to Sophie's parties! Almost everyone joins us.

Sophie doesn't usually invite too many kids to her birthday parties, even with a DJ and horseback riding and funtastic giveaways.

Maybe I should help Jessie and her team. They only have a few kids, and I'm sick of Sophie's nastiness and lying. I should stand up to her. I bite my lip, and I take a step forward.

"Where are you going?" asks Sophie.

"The other team could use help," I say.

"You stay here. Best Friends' Honor."

"What does that even mean?"

"It means you have to stay on my team."

I sigh and stay where I am.

Jessie only has Anna, Seth, Brian, Eddie, and Aaron on her team. I don't see how my team can lose.

Still, after we win, and while I eat my granola bar, I don't think I'll enjoy it much.

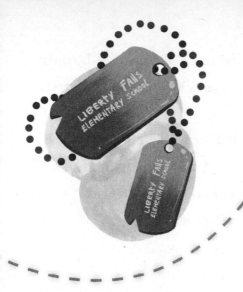

37
AARON

It snowed a ton in Alaska, but I bet this is a record for Liberty Falls.

And to think that last week we wore spring jackets to school. I thought winter was over. I guess I was wrong.

Even though I lived in Alaska, I can still feel today's cold like I'm standing inside a giant Popsicle. Mom says the key to walking around in freezing weather is to wear lots of layers. I've got a fleece jacket under my winter coat and double-insulated gloves.

I found my coat in the entryway where I left it. Poor Eddie's coat was still on that spring-coiled coatrack. It almost grabbed him three times before he was able to snatch it back.

I don't have boots, though. I didn't think to wear boots yesterday. Snow keeps getting into my socks and feet, and I can barely feel my toes. I want to get back inside, hopefully eating granola bars.

But since we're so outnumbered, I think our team is going to be crushed and end up eating cardboard.

Still, I'd rather eat cardboard with my friends than eat granola bars with Sophie.

My friends.

I guess I've made some. It's almost as if Mr. Minks invented a friend-maker, just like I hoped he did.

We get ready for the snowball fight in the back of the house. There are lots of holes in the front of the house, and with all the snow, you could fall in one without even seeing it.

So I suggested we have our fight in the backyard.

And guess what—everyone agreed.

This is even crazier—I'm in charge of our team. It just sort of happened. I told Seth and Brian to build our fort, Jessie and Anna to build a trench around it, and Eddie to help me build snowballs. Everyone nodded and got to work.

I didn't even need a pretend-sergeant voice or anything.

I've picked up some army stuff from Dad. Like, you need to protect yourself before a fight, especially when you are way outmanned. The fort and the trench will do that.

The other team doesn't even bother to build a fort. They think they have won already.

That means we have a chance.

"Let's make these walls thicker," I say to Brian. He and

Seth put large snow mounds into place. We have tall walls. We just need to make them sturdier.

The fort's walls will protect us from direct snowball hits. I punch windows into the middle of the wall. We can throw snowballs out the windows and then duck down to avoid the enemy's fire.

Jessie and Anna finish the trench, which is sort of like a moat. Anyone coming close will fall right in. We can pummel our enemies with snowballs while they try to get out.

It's a good plan. We will stand behind our wall and wait for the enemy to attack. Then they will be sitting ducks.

The other team doesn't build trenches. They spend their time goofing off. A few have started their own snowball fight for fun. Sophie seems to have spent all her time building a giant snow throne to sit on.

"Let's go!" Sophie shouts from her throne. "You guys are wasting time!"

I look at our fort. Our trench. Our snowballs. "We're ready," I shout back.

"Finally!" blares Sophie. "Waiting is dumb. I'll count down from three and we'll start." My team scrambles to get behind the walls of the fort. "Three . . . Fire!"

I should have known Sophie would cheat even when

counting down. We all make it inside our fort, a snowball missing my head by inches.

The other team keeps throwing balls, but they hit our walls and not us. Still, each throw takes a small chip out of our fort, small pieces of ice spraying from the impact. Ball after ball. Chip after chip. They just have so many people and so many snowballs! Part of a wall caves in.

I dash over to patch it back up.

Brian and Seth lob snowballs over our wall or through our windows as fast as they can. They're strong and they can throw far.

I was surprised they picked our team, but Brian said he hates DJs and horseback rides, and so does Seth.

I guess they went to Sophie's party last year and had a lousy time.

Although Brian and Seth can throw far, their aim is terrible. They only hit a couple of kids. Still, that's two kids out.

I pat snow to reinforce our wall to keep it from falling apart. But if I'm patching, I'm not throwing. Next to me, Jessie lobs a snowball high over our wall. It flies and flies and smacks Norm on the nose.

That's one more down for their team.

"Nice shot," I say.

"I've got cat-eye aim," says Jessie with a big smile.

I grab a ball from our dwindling snowball supply—we should have made more—and hurl it through one of the windows I made. It hits Sophie on her foot.

She remains sitting on her snow throne, doing nothing. She doesn't move.

"Hey!" I shout, as loud as I can. "I hit you, Sophie!"

"You missed!" she yells back. But I know I didn't.

A snowball sails over our fort wall and grazes Anna on the shoulder, right when she's about to throw a ball herself. She drops her ball, hangs her head, and sits down. "I'm out," she whispers.

At least our team plays fair.

"Aaron, over here!" shouts Eddie.

I need to patch fort holes and hurl snowballs, and Eddie isn't helping. He waves me to the back of the fort. "Hurry!"

Maybe the other team is trying an ambush. That's what I would do. But I don't think the other team is organized well enough to plan that. Or smart enough.

Or maybe Eddie has a secret plan. Maybe Mr. Minks invented a snowball-making machine or something, and Eddie knows where it is.

"What? We're in the middle of a battle . . ." I stop talking. Eddie points to a set of footprints. They lead around the side of the house.

Those aren't kid footprints, either. They're adult prints. Big adult prints. And they look like they were made here recently, maybe when we were getting ready for the fight.

Whoever walked past us didn't want us to see him or her. The person didn't say anything at all. That's odd.

And next to the footprints is a groove in the snow, like someone dragged something heavy. Such as a large bag.

"Do you think the prints are from one of our teachers?" Eddie asks.

I shake my head.

"Or Mr. St. Clare?"

I shake my head again.

"Or Mr. Felix?"

I nod.

"That's what I thought, too."

We planned to search for inventions and maybe even our classmates after the fight. But this can't wait. This is important.

"Let's grab the rest of the team," I say. They all lob snowballs over the fort.

"They're busy. Just you and me should go," says Eddie. "We'll see what's going on."

"But . . ."

"If we need help, we'll come back. Let's go."

I take a deep breath and nod. We leave to follow the footprints. I feel bad because we shouldn't just abandon our team in the middle of the fight. But finding our classmates and stopping Mr. Felix is more important than winning a granola bar, even if I'm so hungry that eating a box of cardboard doesn't sound as awful as it should.

38
JESSIE

I can't believe we're having a snowball fight to decide breakfast.

When Sophie wouldn't share her granola bars, I threatened to fight her. But there was no way I was going to fight her. I would never fight anyone, not really.

Oscar might fight, but not me.

Actually, I doubt Oscar would fight, either. He looks tough, but my house cat is really very sweet.

I'm glad Chloe suggested a snowball fight, even if we have no chance of winning. Well, maybe we have some chance. Mama says you can do anything if you try hard enough.

I throw balls as fast as I can. I throw them over our wall and through our windows. The other team has way more people than we do. But we have a fort and they don't.

Aaron was pretty smart to build this. But where did he and Eddie go?

My cats always seem to disappear when I need them most, too.

I can't think about Eddie and Aaron—we have a snowball fight to win. Some parts of our wall have caved in from snowballs slamming into it. We can stay behind the parts of the wall that have not caved in. Sophie's team has nothing to protect them.

They are sitting ducks.

Brian and Seth lob ball after ball. Most of them miss everyone, but a few balls hit an arm or a leg. When a kid is hit, they are out.

"Nice!" yells Brian, high-fiving Seth after a direct shot on Kelsey.

We've lost Anna, plus Eddie and Aaron, but Team Sophie is losing people even faster. Then again, they have a lot more kids they can lose.

Sophie looks like she's covered in snow, but she keeps saying, "You missed me!" I don't think that's true.

Two boys from Sophie's team, Cooper and Gavin, storm our fort. They rush forward. They must not see the trench, because they run right into it.

I bombard them with snowballs.

POW! POW! POW!

They are out.

Yes!

The trench was another clever idea from Aaron. I never talked to him before this trip, just like I never talked to Anna.

They both seem pretty awesome. Almost cat-awesome.

Sophie's team still has more kids than us, but not too many more. Seth runs out of the fort. He's armed with a dozen snowballs. He throws them as hard and fast as he can. He shouts, "For granola bars!"

He knocks out four players from the other team in about five seconds. Brian runs out of our fort, too. "Granola bars! Granola bars!"

SPLAT! SPLAT!

Two more of our enemies are knocked out.

It's that fast. Now only three players are left on the other team, including Sophie. This is it! This is when we finish them off! I follow Brian and Seth out of the fort. All three of us whip snowballs.

SPLOOSH! SPLOOSH!

Two more gone.

Only Sophie remains. I take aim. A ball hits her on her shoulder.

"You missed," she says. I throw another snowball. It hits Sophie on the leg. "Missed again!" she hollers.

We all hurl balls. They hit her shoulder, chest, leg, arm, and stomach.

SPLAT! SPLAT! SPLAT! SPLAT! SPLAT!

"Fine. You got me," she says, covered in two inches of snow, frowning deeply.

I high-five Seth. I look at Brian but decide not to return his slap, because his high fives always hurt.

I can't believe we won.

"Granola bars! Granola bars!" Seth and Brian yell.

I yell it, too. "Granola bars!" I'm starving and they sound delicious right now.

We rush into the house, followed by Sophie's team behind us. We shake off our snow and kick off our shoes. Sophie has to practically shimmy like a cat to get all the snow off her.

My socks are soaking wet, so I take them off and rub my feet. It was so cold I can barely feel my toes. Other kids do the same.

I head right to Sophie's bag and dump all the granola bars onto the floor. There are enough for everyone on our team to have at least two. Sophie grunts at me, but then trudges along with the rest of her team to the pile of blueberry muffin cardboard boxes that will be their breakfast.

"Congratulations," says Chloe. "You guys deserved to win." She hangs her head. "Sorry again about Mopey. It just sort of happened." She walks away, her head bowed.

"What were you saying to her? You can't talk to them. Best Friends' Honor!" Sophie says, jabbing her finger at Chloe.

"That's not even a *thing*," says Chloe, walking past Sophie without even looking at her.

Sophie scowls and then nibbles on her cardboard box. "This tastes like gym socks," she complains.

I'm enjoying my chocolate-chip granola bar way too much to care. I'm so hungry I could eat a horse—not that I would. Horses are not as awesome as cats, but they are still pretty awesome.

Horses would be way too big for the animal shelter I'm going to build with Anna and Vivian, though. I wonder if I could get Aaron to help, and maybe Eddie, too.

Aaron and Eddie. Where did they go?

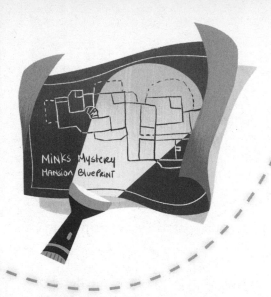

MINKS Mystery MANSION BluePrint

39

EDDIE

We follow the snow prints as they stretch past the house. Whoever made these prints, whether it's Mr. Felix or someone else, has big feet. The prints are easy to walk on. But we still have to move slowly. The snow comes up to my stomach. And the snow is cold against my sneakers.

"Do you think we'll find Principal Klein?" asks Aaron. "Or the missing students?"

I bite my lip and take a deep breath. "I don't know."

"And if Mr. Felix has everyone locked up, what do we do?"

I shake my head. "I still don't know."

But I'm glad we're doing something other than throwing snowballs. We wasted too much time this morning building a fort. I didn't want to leave the group, especially after Jessie and Anna helped us escape the upside-down room last night. But I couldn't stop thinking about the robbery the entire time.

It's time to get to business.

I need to save my legacy.

I just don't know how we can stop the robbery and save our classmates. If anyone can do it, it's me. After all, I'm a Minks.

I shake my head, reminding myself I need to stop thinking like that.

Thinking like that doesn't make any sense.

Trudging around the house through giant mounds of snow makes me realize just how huge and how sprawling the mansion is. Once we pass the middle of the house, the outside keeps changing, as if one day my great-great-great-grandfather wanted to build one kind of house and then a few days later decided to build another. Some parts of the house are brick. Some are made from wood. Others are made with stone.

One room juts out and appears to be held up on stilts.

"I smell pickles," says Aaron.

"The whole place smells like pickles."

"No. I think the smell is coming from around the corner. Actually, it smells sort of good."

I take a big whiff of a roasted pickle smell, like a campfire mixed with pickles. It's not a bad odor at all.

We reach the end of the house. When we do, I stop in my tracks. Or rather, I stop in footprints that are someone else's tracks. Aaron bumps into me because he doesn't realize I'm stopping.

"Sorry," he says.

"Get down," I whisper.

We duck. The snow mound is so tall that when we squat, it's higher than our heads. We're completely hidden.

We peek up, staring.

The footprints veer away from the house and head straight toward a garage. The garage door is raised and a large moving truck sits inside. I can only assume a driveway leads from the garage, but everything is covered with thick snow.

Which means that truck is stuck.

For now.

Next to the truck sits Mr. Felix. He sits on a folding lawn chair roasting pickles on a small grill. The garage looks steamy compared to the frozen air around us.

I stare at the truck. The back door is open, and the truck is half-filled with boxes, some very large as if they held a refrigerator, and some shoe box–sized.

But not everything is in a box, and some things I recognize. I've seen them in books. We saw some in the video Mrs. Greeley played in class.

There's a rocking chair that slowly rocks. That must be Lady Minks's Astonishing Always-Rocking Rocking Chair—a rocking chair that rocks by itself and never stops.

Anyone who sat in it got seasick after a while.

There's also a thin and tall piano—sort of a half piano, but taller. That must be the Minks Terrific Tune Typer. It played music while you typed, which was awesome except it only typed the letters A, B, C, D, E, F, G, and G-flat, and the last one isn't even a letter. Still, the invention is famous. It eventually inspired others to invent the player piano, the electric typewriter, and headphones.

I guess the Terrific Tune Typer didn't sound so terrific.

I also see the Awesome Ah-Choo sitting in the truck. It's basically an oversized yellow telephone.

A lot of people don't know that my great-great-great-grandfather invented the telephone. He built it years before Alexander Graham Bell built his. He never got credit, because every time my ancestor told anyone he built an Awesome Ah-Choo, they gave him a tissue and told him to blow his nose.

My great-great-great-grandfather invented a lot of things that failed. But he never stopped inventing. Some inventions made money. Many didn't. He never cared.

Maybe he was right. Maybe what you do is more important than how much money you make doing it.

Mr. Felix's invention-filled truck is the proof we need that he's trying to steal my great-great-great-grandfather's inventions, even more than those maps and notepad I found. If it wasn't for the snowstorm, the inventions would already be gone.

I can't stand watching this. I turn away.

"Looks like they plan to profit themselves . . . ," begins Aaron.

"And not the world," I say, finishing his sentence.

"He won't stay there grilling pickles forever," says Aaron. "The truck is only half-full. He'll need to come back to the house to steal more stuff. When he comes back, we need to be ready."

"What do you mean?"

"We can build a trap. But we'll need to have everyone working together. And I mean everyone."

I cringe. "Maybe Jessie and Anna can help. They already sort of know some of this. But we don't need anyone else. I'm a Minks, after all."

"Stop doing that," says Aaron, and I hang my head. "My dad says that a platoon working together can do anything. Minks's servants didn't just make meals and do the laundry. They helped build and test the inventions. And, because they helped, Mr. Minks shared his money with them."

My great-great-great-grandfather was generous that way.

Maybe that's one of the reasons why it bothers me that he left us nothing. I would have more money if my great-great-great-grandfather was Minks's butler. But then the Minks name wouldn't be my legacy, and I suppose that's worth a lot, even if my last name is Mudd.

Also, I know Aaron is right. We need as much help as we can get. If the inventions were meant to profit the world, the world needs to step up to protect them.

"Okay," I say. "Thanks."

"For what?"

"For making sense. When we get back, you'll organize the group."

"Me?" Aaron gulps. "You'll do it. It's your family's house."

"It's not my family's house. Liberty Falls owns it. And I'm not good at organizing stuff. You are."

Aaron throws me a look as if I'm as crazy as my great-great-great-grandfather. But I saw how he organized the snow fort. He took control, and it was easy for him. Aaron is a leader, even if he doesn't realize it.

We turn around and follow the footprints back to the house. As we walk, I become more convinced we need everyone to protect the house, at least until our teachers and Principal Klein come back, or until we rescue them if they need to be rescued.

Those thieves will be sorry they messed with Aaron and me.

I mean, those thieves will be sorry they messed with the kids of Liberty Falls Elementary.

40
CHLOE

The front door opens. I eat the final bite of my blueberry muffin cardboard breakfast as a gust of cold air enters the ballroom from the entryway. Eddie and Aaron rush in, kicking snow from their shoes.

"You're getting the floor wet," complains Sophie.

"They're going to steal everything!" shouts Eddie.

"What are you talking about?" Sophie asks, spitting out a small piece of cardboard that's stuck in her teeth.

"The plan! It's true!" Eddie shouts. "Mr. St. Clare and Mr. Felix are stealing inventions. We saw a truck stuffed with them. The only reason they haven't gotten away is because of the storm."

I can't believe that. Mr. St. Clare seems so nice. Sure, Mr. Felix isn't friendly, but maybe he's like me. Maybe he has the wrong friends.

"We need to call the police," says Norm.

The police can always solve everything. There's a phone on the wall near me, so I rush over to it. It's one of those old-fashioned handset phones I've seen in old black-and-white movies that my mom sometimes watches. But when I lift the handle, there's no dial tone. "This doesn't work."

"Who cares?" grumbles Sophie. I frown at her.

"We all should care," says Eddie. "Those inventions are our town's legacy." He puts his hands on his hips. "We need to protect the house."

Jessie stands up. "I'll help." Anna stands up, too.

Sophie would be good at protecting stuff. She's tough and fierce. But she doesn't stand up. She just continues eating her cardboard.

Not too many kids seem interested in helping Eddie. Most kids turn their backs to him and continue chomping on their breakfasts.

"I know, profiting the world seems like a waste of time," says Eddie. "At least I thought so. But I was wrong. Minks's inventions were incredible. And maybe great things, things that really matter, should be for everyone and not just to make a few people rich."

Sophie rolls her eyes. I can tell she's paying attention but just doesn't care.

I care.

"Eddie is right," says Aaron. "I know. What's the big deal about a bunch of old inventions and weird pickle stuff? Mr. Minks was strange. But he made a big difference, and history is important. It's what brings us together. If Mr. St. Clare and Mr. Felix steal this stuff, then what happens to the town? This house and his inventions are part of what makes Liberty Falls special. I mean, I've only lived here for a short time, but even I know that."

Kids have stopped eating. Everyone looks at Aaron.

"We'll all have to work together," he says. "Principal Klein says we're responsible, but I don't think he believes it. But he should. We can make a difference. If all of us work together, we can save our history." He smiles at Eddie, and Eddie smiles back. "We can protect this house, as a team. One team."

"It's just a shame I don't have my cats here to help," says Jessie.

"Count me in," says Seth.

"Me too," says Brian.

Other kids shout as well. Norm stands up, and so does Wesley. Then everyone stands. We all want to help.

Well, not everyone. Sophie hasn't moved.

But I'm super excited to pitch in. "I want to help!" I say, waving my hand. You're always supposed to wave your hand when you talk in groups.

"I'm not helping anyone," says Sophie. "And neither are you. Sit down."

I stop and look at Sophie. She sneers, cardboard in her teeth.

I can choose to be like Sophie and sit down and not help, or I can choose to be who I want to be.

It's time I start acting like the person I want to be. I take a step forward.

"One more step and you won't be my friend or be invited to my party," says Sophie.

I stop and slip the best friend necklace from around my head. I look at it and sigh. Then I turn and look back at Sophie. "I'm sorry." I take a deep, deep breath. Sophie relaxes, but I'm not done. "I'm sorry, but I hope you have a nice birthday party this year. I guess I won't be going. And you have my word on that. Best Friends' Honor, too."

As I put the necklace in my pocket and join the other kids, I feel pretty rotten for saying that to Sophie.

But I also feel sort of good.

I also feel that maybe I should have stopped listening to Sophie a long time ago and not just now.

41
AARON

If my dad were here, I know he'd have a better plan, an army plan, but I've done a pretty excellent job, I think. I have our whole anti-burglar contraption mapped out on notebook paper.

It will work.

I think.

Brian and Seth walk up to me with a big pile of wooden slats and poles. Many look like they were torn from walls and who knows what. "We found these," says Brian.

"Um, where did you find them?" I ask. A lump forms in my throat.

"Attached to things."

There are nails on some of the slats pieces. I try to imagine what they might have been attached to.

We're trying to protect the house, not destroy it.

"I don't know if we can use any of this stuff," I tell them.

"But do you think you can find those bowling balls again? The extra-light and powerful ones?"

"I think so," said Brian.

"Just be careful," I warn. "Don't break anything else!"

Jessie stands behind me, waiting for direction. "We need grease," I tell her. "Or something slippery."

"There's a big barrel of pickle juice near the kitchen. It's pretty smelly, but I bet it's very slippery, too."

"That sounds perfect."

"Do we need a jar of one-hundred-and-fifty-year-old pickles? I can grab those, too." I nod, and Jessie rushes off with Anna.

All this time, Sophie sits in the corner, her arms folded, frowning at everyone. She's the only kid not helping.

We don't need her. Let her frown.

The rest of us work together. We should have been working together from the start. We never should have had a snowball fight over breakfast.

We make a pretty good platoon.

There are plenty of tools here, mixed up with broken metal and cracked gear from the fallen Invention Table. Norm grabs a screwdriver to disconnect the light switch in the front hall. He says his dad is an electrical engineer and he's done this sort of thing before. He even knew how to shut off the power first. I would have no idea how to do that.

Wesley pushes a large blue stainless-steel machine across the room. It's on wheels, so it's easy to move, but it must have been hard to lug it here. I show him where to place it.

"I'll set it up," Wesley says. "I know what to do."

Jessie and Anna push the barrel of pickle juice toward me. Some of the liquid splashes over the sides. It has a terrible stink, much worse than I thought. My eyes water even though I stand a few feet away from it.

"That's messed up," I groan.

"I know," says Jessie. "Just be glad you're not a cat. Their sense of smell is twice as powerful as people's. But if my cats were here, I'd sic them on those bad guys. They wouldn't know what hit them."

"I doubt they'll know what hit them anyway," I say.

"True, but it would be easier with cats."

I don't know how much time we have, though. We need to have our defenses up before Mr. Felix arrives, and we still have a lot to do.

But when he comes back in, he'll be sorry.

We continue setting up our trap. Norm finishes disconnecting the light switch. We need the room to be dark. Although, if things go right, the room will be very dark for Mr. Felix even with the lights on.

Brian and Seth wander back into the room. They each hold two bowling balls. Brian stumbles. The balls slip out of his arms, but he gathers them back to his chest before they fall on the floor.

"I only dropped one upstairs," he says. "It put a hole in the floor, but you can barely notice it, as long as you avoid the floor."

"What should we do with these?" asks Seth.

"Put them down—carefully! Brian, can you help Eddie prepare the net? And, Seth, can you find your way back to the workshop and get the Amazing Almost Forever Paste? Hurry."

They rush off.

"Seth—grab the Never Forever Spray, too! And, guys—don't break anything!"

I keep my fingers crossed.

I check off the items on my list. I ask Anna to grab a mop from the kitchen. But the clock is ticking. Mr. Felix could be back any moment.

If he gets back before we're done, then none of the inventions will be safe—at least none of the inventions we haven't busted ourselves.

42

JESSIE

I peek over Aaron's shoulder as he stands at the end of the entryway. He studies the designs he drew. I bet Aaron will be a famous inventor when he grows up. His ideas are pretty awesome.

His trap reminds me a little of the game Mouse Trap, which is a game I love, because when I think of mice, I think of Patches.

He and Eddie will be wonderful additions to ART.

Animals Rock, Totally! And so do friends.

We're getting close to being done with our trap. I can't believe we made this whole thing so quickly.

When our entire class works together, we can get a lot done.

But I still don't know what happened to the rest of us or our missing teachers. I hope they're okay.

"Are we ready?" I ask Aaron.

"Almost. We just need Seth to get back with that Almost Forever Paste."

I rush off to help Norm adjust the meal catapult, and watch as everyone puts the last few pieces of our plan into place. A couple of kids hang sheets over the entryway windows so the room will be dark. Eddie sets the net on the ground.

Seth runs into the room. "I have the paste and the spray!"

But instead of handing the paste to Aaron, Seth flips the tube to him. Aaron has to step to the side to catch it, and he bangs into the giant, smelly vat of pickle juice.

It topples over with a loud CRZNNGG!

Oozing pickle juice spills onto the floor. It rolls all the way to the front door.

Norm shouts. "Someone's coming! Everyone! Hide!"

We run to the side of the room, out of sight. Aaron steps on the pickle juice. It's very slippery and he almost falls, but he wiggles his arms and keeps his balance. He comes over to me and squirts the Amazing Almost Forever Paste on the white sheets draped over the clothesline.

Anna, standing on the other side of the room, flips a light switch. The entryway grows dark.

I stand as still as a cat, ready to do my part. Fen can stand still for a long time, and so can I.

No one says a word. I'm not sure if anyone even breathes.

The doorknob turns.

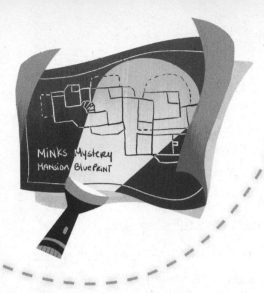

MINKS MYSTERY
MANSION BLUEPRINT

43

EDDIE

The door opens, and two men walk into the house and close the door. A tiny bit of light shines through the blankets covering the windows, but it's too dark to see much. I can't see the faces of the men.

But it must be Mr. Felix and Mr. St. Clare. Who else could it be?

They are here to steal our town's history. But they are about to be in for a big surprise.

One of the men hits the light switch. But it doesn't turn on, thanks to Norm.

"Odd, the light doesn't work," says one of the men. "If only I had a lighter, then I could make this room lighter." That must be Mr. St. Clare talking.

The men take off their winter coats and boots and step forward. They are now standing in their socks, and the entryway is covered with pickle juice. Very, very slippery pickle juice.

"What is this?" asks Mr. St. Clare. "And why does this house smell like pickle juice?"

He starts to slip as soon as he steps forward, but instead of falling, he does a small hop. The second man does not hop. He flails. His feet fly up. He hangs in the air for a moment and then crashes down on his back with a painful—

CRACK!

But he doesn't stop where he fell. Instead he slides, the pickle juice as slippery as ice, and he barrels into the other thief headfirst.

The second man falls on top of the first man.

"Ow! . . . Hey! . . . Get off me!" cries a murmur of voices.

One of the men staggers up. As soon as he stands, his feet immediately fly out from under him again, and he falls on top of the other man, who was just starting to get up, too.

"We better put on the brakes before we break our necks!" yells Mr. St. Clare.

Yes, that's definitely Mr. St. Clare.

Both men try to stand. "Be careful!" warns Mr. St. Clare. They walk forward, slowly. It's dark in here, so they can't see anything well.

They don't notice the clothesline hanging across the room. How could they? It would be almost invisible even with the lights on.

Anna stands on the other side of the room. As the men

approach the clothesline, she pulls a rope toward her. White sheets slide across the line, and to the middle of the room.

The men walk right into the white sheets. The sheets cling to them, draping over their heads.

Since Aaron spread them with Almost Forever Paste, those sheets aren't coming off. The two men yank on the sheets, trying to pull them off, but there is no way they are budging.

With sheets covering their heads, the men look like two ghosts.

The room was already dark, but now I doubt the two men can see anything at all.

Their arms moving around to feel where they are, and to keep their balance on the slippery pickle-juice-puddle floor, the would-be robbers bang their heads together.

KA-CRSSHH!

Both men fall, once again landing on top of each other.

I let out a small laugh, and then quickly put my hand to my mouth. Everything is going perfectly. Those crooks deserve every bump for trying to steal our town's history.

The two sheet-pasted ghosts stand up, woozy, and wobble back and forth.

One of the men slips on the juice and spins backward. He puts his arms out to steady himself. He bangs right into the Sensational Spring-Coiled Coatrack.

I pushed it, very carefully, closer to the middle of the room.

As soon as the man touches it, the machine springs into action, grabbing his clothes and lifting him into the air.

"Hey! Let me go!" the man cries, kicking and squirming.

His voice is muddled under the sheet covering his head. But I don't think it sounds like Mr. Felix. It's hard to tell for sure.

Still, a small lump forms in my stomach.

If that's not Mr. Felix, who is it?

The man's clothing rips in half. I can hear the threads pulling and tearing. As he falls to the ground, another arm from the coatrack reaches out toward him. The man scrambles away, just out of its reach.

But we still have plenty of tricks waiting.

The man dashing from the coatrack slips on the juice again. His feet fly up, and he rams into the second thief. They both skid forward, sliding like two ice cubes, and run right into a string tied across the room. The string snaps in half.

The string is attached to a switch. The switch is attached to the Minks Breathtaking Balloon Machine.

Immediately, sixty-two water balloons expand.

The sound of expanding rubber and rushing water fill the room.

"What do we hear, here?" asks Mr. St. Clare.

Meanwhile, the machine ties off the end of each balloon. The balloons drop into a trench and slide down, landing at the feet of Brian and Seth.

They're ready.

They both launch balloon after balloon after balloon.

Sixty-two water balloons sail in the air, two by two by two.

It looks like throwing all those snowballs earlier was good practice. They have much better aim now.

SPLAT! SPLAT! SPLAT! SPLAT!

Sixty-two times.

Some balloons miss, but most of them smash into the men. The thieves, now soaked and dripping water, stagger back, bumping into each other again, and then crash to the ground.

THUNK!

"Get me out of here!" shouts one of the men, rising slowly from the ground.

Meanwhile, the other man gets up, wobbles to his left, and steps right on top of the *X* we taped to the floor. That's the cue for Norm.

"Now!" Aaron screams.

"Who's there?" asks the man.

Norm releases the meal catapult sitting in the corner, armed with dozens of 150-year-old pickles.

The rope goes TWANG!

The shower of pickles goes WHOOSH!

The wet and slimy pickles soar across the room and splatter on top of the thieves.

The men fall from the onslaught of ancient vegetables. Their heads bonk together again. They crash to the floor.

One of them moves, slowly. Then the other one moans, and then asks, "Um, what's that noise?"

We can all hear it.

It's a roaring sound.

A loud sound.

The sound of four surprisingly light but very powerful balls rolling straight toward the men, bowled by Brian and Seth.

The room is filled with the loud echo of the Ludicrously Light Bowling Balls moving closer and closer.

Rolling.

Rolling.

At the last second the balls curve, as if each followed a wet patch of pickle juice. The balls just miss the men and ram into the wall behind them.

BAM! POW! CRASH!

Four large holes appear in the far wall.

"Whoops," says Seth.

"What crashed?" shouts one of the men.

The other man staggers up. "I don't know, but let's get out of this room!"

The men manage to get across the floor without slipping, heading toward the ballroom.

But before they get there, they run right on top of the net I laid down.

As soon as they step on it—TWANG!

The net springs up. It wraps itself around the men. And then it bounds up into the air, swinging under the staircase.

The men grunt and groan, trapped inside the net.

"We did it!" cries Aaron. "We captured the robbers!"

Our entire group lets out a loud cheer.

"We captured someone. But are you sure they are robbers?" asks Jessie. Her voice sounds uncertain.

As Aaron turns on the light switch, I have a bad feeling about this.

44

CHLOE

No one seems super happy, but I don't understand why. We won! We defeated the bad guys! Maybe we'll get medals!

Oh. Never mind.

Now I see why no one is super happy.

Principal Klein stares down at us from inside the giant net. At least I think that's our principal—he's covered with a sheet, but you can't miss his bright orange cardigan sweater. He and the other guy, who must be Mr. St. Clare, are sort of tangled, their arms and legs twisted together like two pretzels.

My stomach feels all jumpy. What have we done?

Aaron mists Never Forever Spray on the sheets, and the linens slide right off.

Principal Klein glares at us, his eyes bulging. I've never seen him this angry before. "Let me out of here!" he demands. "What is the meaning of this?"

Seth has already grabbed an old pair of scissors from the pile of invention stuff on the ground. He cuts through the bottom of the net. The net slowly tears, then splits open all at once.

BASH! CRUNCH! Both Mr. St. Clare and Principal Klein tumble out, landing on top of each other and onto the hard marble floor.

"My head!" Principal Klein cries. He sits up and shakes dirt from his sleeve. His sweater is ripped in half. His head is covered with scrapes and scratches. He is dripping wet from water balloons and also coated in pickle slime. I wonder if he'll ever be able to wash away the pickle stink that oozes from him.

He starts to stand, but wobbles and sits.

"Not so fast," says Brian, walking up to Principal Klein and pointing down. "We've caught you thieves, and we're not letting you get away."

"What are you talking about?" Principal Klein says. His tone is snappish and angry.

"Where have you been all night?" demands Brian.

"Inside the milking barn and stables," Principal Klein says. "By the time we found Mrs. Welp, Mrs. Rosenbloom, and the other students, it was dark and snowing too hard to get back. The milking barn is heated, so we spent the night and made roasted pickles for dinner. They were delicious. In fact, Mrs. Welp and the children should be back here any minute. I'm not sure what's taking them so long."

"Oh," says Brian, stepping back. "Then, never mind." He keeps stepping back until he's hiding behind Seth.

Mr. St. Clare sits up and groans. "How many days have I been out? I'm all in a daze."

"You've only been on the ground for a minute," Principal Klein replies. To us he snaps, "But what's this about a robbery?"

"We thought you were robbers trying to steal some of the inventions," says Eddie. "We wanted to protect the house."

"Mr. St. Clare and Mr. Felix plan to steal everything," adds Aaron. "I'm sorry we trapped you, Principal Klein, but we saw Mr. St. Clare's notes. Jessie heard him talking. We saw Mr. Felix stealing inventions. Those two thieves thought they could get away with their plan, but we couldn't let that happen."

I've been slinking, unseen in the back, but Aaron's words make me lift my head. He's right. We shouldn't be sorry for what we did.

We weren't being mean. We were standing up for ourselves, and for what we believed in.

We were standing up for our town.

I guess Principal Klein is innocent, but Mr. St. Clare is not!

"History is important," adds Eddie. "Our town's legacy depended on our stopping the robbery. We're just sorry we caught you, too."

Principal Klein gasps. "Is that true?" He faces Mr. St. Clare, his mouth wide open in shock.

Mr. St. Clare shakes his head. He still appears a little woozy. He has a big welt on his forehead. "Of course not." He rubs his bump gently, wincing. "Oh, this painful knot!"

"But we saw the inventions in a truck," says Eddie.

"Yes. We are sending them off for a nationwide tour of Mr. Minks's life," says Mr. St. Clare.

"It's been in all the papers," Principal Klein adds. "There was a big announcement last week."

What have we done?

"But I overheard you," says Jessie. "You said you were looking for secret inventions."

"That's true," says Mr. St. Clare. "Just imagine how many people would want to see the tour then. If we found secret inventions and especially Minks's fabled lost notebook—the Mysterious Machines of Mr. Minks—the house would be saved."

"Saved?" asks Eddie.

Mr. St. Clare sighs. "I hate to talk about it. Just thinking about the tour reminds me of how much money we need to pour into the poor mansion. It's old and in need of repair. Even the windowpanes are a pain to maintain."

"Is that why you kept changing the subject whenever we asked about missing things?" I ask.

"So you noticed?" asks Mr. St. Clare. "And I thought I was being so clever." He sighs. "By the way, did you know Mr. Minks invented a Tee Bag? Golfers could play a round of golf and then make a hot beverage. Unfortunately, playing golf would always leave a hole in one."

"You're changing the subject again," says Principal Klein.

"Sorry, force of habit," says Mr. St. Clare.

The floor is still slippery with pickle juice. I step back, slip, and bang into Anna. We both fall. Pickle juice soaks my pants.

Norm already has grabbed the mop and scrubs the floor. He mops the area around us. When I stand up, it's less slippery.

But mopping up pickle juice won't mop us out of trouble. From the look on Principal Klein's face, we're already in way more trouble than I can even imagine.

We just wanted to do a good deed.

Principal Klein looks around the room. We all do. There are bits of shattered picture frames, piles of broken wood, and scattered gears and metal pieces. There are four large bowling ball holes in one of the walls. And I know there is damage in lots of other rooms and not just this one.

"I thought you wanted to save the house. It looks like you destroyed it," Principal Klein says.

The house is certainly not funtastic. Not anymore, at least.

"In protecting it we may have accidentally damaged a few things," admits Seth.

"A few things?" Principal Klein's face is bright red. "Is there anything you didn't destroy?"

"Hopefully," says Eddie.

Mr. St. Clare shakes as he looks around the room. His voice quivers. "We couldn't afford the sum to fix even some of these things," he mumbles. "I hate to say it, but even with a tour, I fear all is lost."

"What do you mean?" asks Principal Klein.

"Must I mention the words? The money from the tour could have restored the mansion. But now? Without the Mysterious Machines of Mr. Minks, we could never raise enough money to fix the fix we're in. The house is as good as closed. Forever."

I don't know whose face is whiter, Mr. St. Clare's or Eddie's. Eddie, who seemed so sure of himself just a few minutes ago, is as pale as a ghost, or at least as pale as someone dressed in a white sheet pretending to be a ghost. He breathes heavily, leaning over as if trying to catch his breath.

"You kids—you've ruined everything," says Mr. St. Clare, tears falling down his frowning face. "By and by, we'll all now have to say bye-bye to the Minks Mystery Mansion."

45
AARON

We stand around Principal Klein and Mr. St. Clare. No one says a word. I can't believe that instead of saving the house we nearly destroyed it. None of us can. I take a deep breath and step forward. "This is all my fault."

"Yours?" Principal Klein stares at me.

"I designed the trap. I was the leader of the group." In the army, generals take responsibility for a mission's success, not privates. I was in charge.

I may not have wanted to be a leader, but I was.

"Very responsible of you," Principal Klein says. "But it's everyone's fault. All of you contributed to this disaster."

The door opens and Kyle jogs in, along with a gust of wind and a flurry of snow blown in from outside.

"We made it!" says Kyle, shaking off snow. He raps, "We tried to get back last night but weren't able. So we spent the night in a stable." He holds Soda in his hands. "We learned a lot about milking and dairy. Still, this poor girl found it all pretty scary."

The rest of the missing kids trudge through the doors right behind him, kicking snow from their shoes.

"Sorry it took us so long," says Mrs. Welp. She and Mrs. Rosenbloom walk into the mansion. "I fell in seven holes."

"But we got her out," adds Mrs. Rosenbloom.

"I don't understand," says Principal Klein, scratching his head. "All you had to do was follow our footsteps."

"I thought I saw footsteps heading to those holes," explains Mrs. Welp. "Apparently, I was mistaken."

As Eddie might say, some people just don't make any sense.

Mrs. Rosenbloom looks around the room. "What happened here?" Her eyes go wide as she sees all the mess and wall holes we made.

"It's a long story," groans Jessie.

Maggie, Paige, and Lacey walk up to Principal Klein. Each holds a piece of paper. "We did our reports," Maggie says.

For a moment, Principal Klein looks confused, but then he nods and takes their reports. "Right. The essays. I'm sure everyone who stayed in this house did their reports as I asked." He holds his hands out.

No one moves.

"Your reports?" Principal Klein looks around, and when no one says anything, he sounds even angrier. "None of you who stayed here last night wrote an essay, as I asked?"

"We thought we'd find the hidden inventions," admits Seth. "And we'd get an A-plus no matter what."

"And then we were busy trying to stop you from stealing things," says Brian. Principal Klein glares down at him. "Or we thought we were stopping you."

Principal Klein shakes his head. His face turns even redder, so that it looks sort of like a giant tomato face. His hands, he has big hands, are clenched tightly. "So. All you did last night was destroy this house?"

"Actually, we did most of the destroying this morning," I squeak in a slightly terrified voice. You don't mess with Principal Klein. His voice is loud enough when he talks at regular volume, but it gets even louder when he's mad.

I sneak a peek at Eddie. I don't think I've seen anyone so miserable. His lips quiver and his eyes water. He sniffles.

I feel terrible, too. I know this isn't my great-great-great-grandfather's house, but the entire trap was my idea. Despite what Principal Klein said, I was responsible.

Principal Klein shakes his head. "I can't imagine a worse fifth grade anywhere in the world. Everyone who stayed in the house is responsible for this disaster. I have no choice. Everyone in Mrs. Greeley's class is expelled from school."

Loud shouts fill the room, spilling from the mouths of the kids who helped protect the house, or thought we were protecting the house.

"You can't do that!" shouts Norm.

"I didn't destroy everything, only some things," whines Wesley.

"What about middle school next year, can we still go?"

"It's not fair!"

"But I ate cardboard! Isn't that punishment enough?"

"Since we're not in Mrs. Greeley's class, are we expelled?" asks Brian.

"Yes, you two, too," answers Principal Klein. Despite the look of gloom on his face, Mr. St. Clare's mouth curls slightly upward.

"I wasn't involved at all," says Sophie. "Expel the rest of them if you want. But I didn't help build that dumb trap."

Mr. St. Clare's small smile quickly goes away, and is replaced by the biggest frown I've ever seen. He bites his fingernails. He picks up slats of wood from the ground and trembles. He wanders to the wall and traces the outline of one of the gaping bowling ball holes. "Ruined. All ruined!" he moans. "We were going to call the tour *The Upside-Down Tour*, since the inventor wanted to turn the world upside down."

That's when it hits me.

The upside-down room.

The clue from the lab.

Why didn't I think of it before? It all makes sense.

"What time is it?" I blurt out.

Principal Klein looks at his watch. "Nine fifty," he says. "Why?"

Because we still have a chance to save the mansion.

46

JESSIE

"The hidden room! Come on!" Aaron shouts to Eddie, running. Eddie is right behind him. Anna and I follow, too.

"Where are you going?" Principal Klein demands. "Come back here!"

Aaron skids on a puddle of pickle juice, and so do I. Somehow we don't fall. Aaron sprints up the grand stairway. I'm only a step behind.

"I demand you come back this instant!" shouts Principal Klein from below.

We don't stop. We follow Aaron.

He runs down the hall, turns the corner, and stops at the closet that leads to the upside-down room. I don't know what's going on, but my heart is pounding.

Aaron opens the door. "I need a hand."

I cup my hands and give Aaron a boost up. He twists the

lightbulb, and the door in back opens. The four of us crawl through.

As soon as we all get into the room, the panel closes behind us.

We're standing on the ceiling again. I'm panting from running so fast.

"What time is it?" asks Aaron.

I look at the clock on the wall, but it's upside down so sort of hard to read. I have to turn my head a little. "Nine fifty-six."

"Do you remember what the inventor wrote in his lab?" asks Aaron.

"Of course." Eddie repeats the rhyme I haven't thought about since yesterday morning:

"Start work at 1
And you won't have any fun.
But start work at 01
And you'll have a ton!"

"Exactly," Aaron says. "I knew it was a clue. I thought *01* referred to army time, like *zero one hundred*, which means one a.m."

Eddie nods. "That made sense. Except it didn't tell us where to look, only when to look. And one a.m. passed a long time ago."

"I thought he wrote *01* instead of *zero one hundred* because hardly anything rhymes with *hundred*," says Aaron.

"*None said*," says Anna quietly. "That rhymes with *hundred*. And so does *fun bed*."

"I'm not sure if those can help us find the secret clue," says Eddie.

"Anyway, what if I had it all wrong?" asks Aaron. "Look at the backward clock. What does the *10* look like, when it's upside down?"

"*01*," I say, looking at the clock.

Aaron smiles. "Exactly. I don't know why I didn't think of that before. So maybe there is a secret room but it can only be found here, in this room, at ten a.m.?"

"That works with the rhyme," I say.

"And Mr. St. Clare said that Minks wanted to create inventions that turned the world upside down," Aaron points out. "And we couldn't figure out why he invented an upside-down room in the first place."

"It's ten now," says Anna, pointing at the clock. "Or upside down, *01* o'clock."

I hold my breath, waiting for something to move, to creak, or a hole to appear somewhere. This could be it. This could be when we find the secret invention.

Nothing happens.

But.

A small stream of light shoots in from the window, almost like a laser beam. The light hits the upside-down mirror, right square in the middle.

The laser stream of light doesn't bounce directly off the mirror, like it would reflect off a regular mirror. It sort of twists and hits the far wall at an odd angle. Maybe the upside-down mirror was created not to be upside down, but to reflect the light exactly like that.

It shines on a small spot in the far wall.

Aaron runs over to the spot and runs his hand on the wall. "I feel something here. I think there's a button."

I squint. I can't see a thing. The button must be hidden under the wallpaper. You would never know it was there unless you knew the clue and saw the beam of light. I don't even think Patches could have found it.

Aaron pushes the wall just as the beam of light starts to fade away. As soon as he presses it, rusty clacking and clinking fill the room. The entire wall rises up as if pulled by ancient chains.

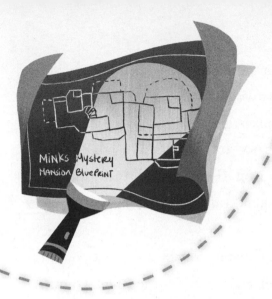

47

EDDIE

We walk into a room, and I'm absolutely positive this was not in any blueprint or map or history book I've seen.

I can barely take a breath I'm so excited. The room is crammed with stuff that makes my head swim. I can't imagine what some of these things do. There are dozens of inventions, like a microscope on large metal legs, an ironing board on stilts, and a bunch of rubber faces stuck together—it was rumored that my great-great-great-grandfather invented masking tape, and here's the proof.

There are lots of boxes and crates, too, many piled on top of one another. Anna opens a box and lifts a hand tool that's the shape of an ape. "What's this?"

"A monkey wrench?" I guess.

"Check this out!" yells Jessie. She holds a four-foot horse that seems to be made entirely of tissue paper.

"An origami horse. Cool," says Aaron.

Jessie presses the origami's horse head, and it yells, "Neigh!" and then runs across the room.

As the others open boxes, I stare at the giant desk in the middle of the room. On top of the desk is a book, a huge notebook as long as my arm. The book is thick, too, with dozens and dozens of papers stuffed inside it, some partially sticking out.

As I open the book, my hands tremble.

Every page in the book appears to have a detailed drawing of a different invention, all with handwritten details and notes. I flip through the titles: Boomerang Toasters, Self-Healing Moccasins, Toe Cakes, Electric Burps, and a whole bunch of things involving pickles. This book must be priceless.

I grab the book and cradle it to my body. "We have to show everyone," I say. "We have to show everyone the secret room exists and the mansion is saved."

I want to share these ideas with everyone. The entire world will benefit from my great-great-great-grandfather's brilliance.

Well, I'm not sure if the world will profit from Fortune-Telling Swordfish Kabobs—I have no idea what those even are—but who knows?

It's easy to find our way back. Hugging the book to my chest, we walk out of the secret room, back into the upside-down room, and jump into the trash can, one at a time. I jump first.

A few moments later, I come tumbling out of the chute. Every kid stares down at their feet, and Principal Klein's face is bright red.

I think we missed a lot of yelling.

After I fall into the room, I move out of the way as Aaron, Jessie, and Anna tumble out, one at a time. Principal Klein and all our schoolmates stare at us.

Principal Klein's voice is loud and angry. He wags his finger at us. "Where do you think you went? What is the meaning of this?"

"We found it!" I say, bouncing to my feet. "The room with the secret inventions! It exists. And look! It's Mr. Minks's own mystery notebook. It's filled with hundreds, if not thousands, of inventions."

"The room is amazing," adds Aaron.

"It is," says Anna, but in such a soft whisper I can barely hear her.

"It even has a paper horse that comes alive," says Jessie. "And so many other incredible things."

Principal Klein looks stunned. So does Mr. St. Clare. His mouth is open so wide you could throw a pickle in it.

"Do you know what this means?" asks Mr. St. Clare.

"That those guys all get A-pluses on their essays?" asks Brian.

Mr. St. Clare runs up to me. He's trembling. He gently takes the book from me. He traces his finger over the cover. "This means the house is saved. The book! *The Mysterious Machines of Mr. Minks*. It exists." His eyes look wet. "I'm so happy, I could turn the ballroom into a bawl room."

Principal Klein clears his throat. "Well, that's wonderful news. Simply incredible." I beam, but then I guess the shock of seeing us return goes away, because he shakes his head and his forehead furrows. "But finding that book does not turn back time. It does not forgive the destruction you caused in this house. The inventions you destroyed. I suppose expelling all of you is a bit severe. But you will all need to write an essay on the importance of respecting valuable property. I will also be speaking with your parents and guardians about you volunteering your time to repair this house."

The punishment doesn't seem so bad, considering what we did. I would have volunteered to help clean up the house anyway. I'm a Minks, after all. I might not be better than anyone else, but I do have a responsibility to uphold my great-great-great-grandfather's incredible legacy.

"Can we partner with someone to write our essays?" Brian asks.

"I guess so," says Principal Klein.

Aaron smiles at me. Of course we'll be essay-writing partners.

Mr. St. Clare hugs the book as tears fall from his cheeks. "The broken inventions are a shame, but this book means everything. It means we won't have to close the mansion."

For a moment, I picture myself as rich as I've ever imagined. I think of how the Minks name won't just live on in history books, but my family can live in our own mansion with a huge entryway and the world's largest ceiling fan.

Although, actually, I kind of like my bedroom. I don't need a bigger one.

You can't put a price on history. Maybe my family can keep some money, enough so the bank won't take our house. But most of it should go toward restoring this house. Forever.

That will be my legacy. Our family's legacy.

Minks was right. Profiting the world is way better than profiting yourself.

48

CHLOE

Everyone jumps around and high-fives one another. Brian keeps slapping people's hands as hard as he can, and he hits hard. WHACK! SMACK! Some kids hold their hands after his slaps, so I stay away from him.

Sophie stands in the corner, not high-fiving anyone. I think maybe I should run over to her, but instead I stay where I am.

What's the opposite of funtastic? Un-funtastic? *That's* Sophie.

But the rest of us are happy. I think the happiest is Eddie, who hugs everyone. Most of us usually sort of ignore him, but not today. Lots of kids have always found him annoying, but maybe he's not anymore. He's sort of a hero, and so are Aaron, Jessie, and Anna.

I hope I'm invited to *their* birthday parties.

A sound blares from outside, an engine gunning like from a loud lawn mower or garbage truck. I look out the window, where a huge snowplow—the biggest I've ever seen—drives up to the house, clearing snow from the driveway.

The driver sticks his head out the window. It's Mr. Felix. He smiles, a lopsided tooth-missing smile, and it doesn't even look creepy.

I guess we won't be trapped in this house for a long time, after all.

"Everyone, gather your things and stand with your trip buddy," says Principal Klein. He puts down a cell phone. It looks like phone service is working again. "That was Mrs. Frank from the school. The streets are cleared and the buses should be here in a few minutes."

I look over to my trip buddy. Sophie isn't even packing her gear. She sits in the corner nibbling blueberry muffin cardboard and frowning. I start to wave to her, but stop myself.

Instead, I tap Anna's shoulder. "I don't have a trip buddy anymore. Can I join you guys?"

"Of course," says Jessie.

I hope she and Anna will forgive me for helping Sophie be so mean. But from the friendly smiles on their faces, maybe they already have.

A few minutes later, we're boarding the school bus. I sit down with Anna on one side of me, and Jessie on the other. I catch Aaron's eye and wave to him. He waves back, and so does Eddie.

"You both should come over after dinner tonight. We can work on our essays together," says Jessie to Anna and me.

"Can I bring Mopey?" asks Anna. "Would your cats mind?"

"My cats are all sweethearts. Patches and Mopey will be best friends—I know it. My cats have excellent taste," says Jessie.

"I can write the essay," I say. "And you guys can copy off me."

Jessie laughs. "Why would you do that?"

That's a good question. I'm not sure if I can even answer it. It's just what I've always done with Sophie. "I'm glad I got to know you guys. Maybe someday I'll be as brave as you, Jessie."

"My cats are brave, not me."

I laugh. "You're super brave! You challenged Sophie when no one else would, including me. You volunteered to go into that dark basement, even though you didn't have to. You always stand up for yourself and for others. You're the bravest person I know."

"Stop it. I'm not," says Jessie. "I just pretend to be that way sometimes. All that stuff scares me."

"That makes you even braver," says Anna. "Everyone gets frightened. It's doing stuff when you're scared that makes you extra brave."

"I never thought of that," says Jessie. "I bet even my cats get scared sometimes, even when they don't show it."

Anna nods.

Jessie and Anna are really smart.

"My mom says that actions speak louder than words," I say. "I've been thinking a lot about that. Like, just because you *think* you're nice doesn't mean you *are* nice if you don't *act* nice. I wasn't very nice to you guys. Sorry."

"I think you're nice," says Anna in a soft voice. "At least, I think you're nice now."

"Me too," says Jessie.

"Really? Best Friends' Honor?" I ask.

"What's that?" asks Jessie. "Is that really a *thing*?"

I laugh. "I'm not sure!"

I peek at Aaron and Eddie. Aaron always acted quiet, but when we needed a leader, he stepped up. He was always that way—he just never showed it. Eddie always acted like a jerk. But he's not, and now we know that, too.

Mom is right. How we act is way more important than what we think deep down inside.

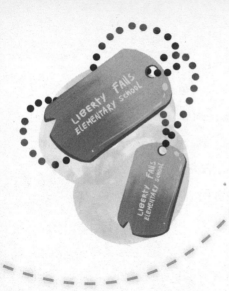

49
AARON

As we wait in line to board the bus, Eddie stands next to me. He no longer has that smug look he always seemed to have before our trip. Maybe he's lost it forever. He smiles at me, and I smile back.

I would have said it was a totally crazy idea two days ago—but I think Eddie is my new best friend.

"Want to come over tonight and write our essays together?" Eddie asks.

"Let me check my schedule," I say, and Eddie frowns. "Just kidding. Of course."

We're next to climb aboard the bus. We run up the steps and grab a seat near the middle. Chloe smiles and waves to us, and we wave back.

I have lots of new friends.

Seth and Brian sit in front of us. Seth turns around. "Your great-great-great-grandfather was amazing," he says to Eddie.

"A genius," adds Brian.

"I know," says Eddie, puffing out his cheeks. He then blushes a little and says, "I mean, thanks. I think so, too. I'm lucky to be related to him."

Eddie leans back with a giant grin. I don't remember ever seeing him smile before this field trip, and now I can't imagine him without one. "It all worked out, huh?" he says. "Do you know my parents have never been to this house? That doesn't make any sense, does it? I'll need to bring them. There are going to be a whole bunch of new inventions to check out soon."

We lean back on our seats. I feel very tired. As the school bus doors close, I think about taking a nap when I get home. But mostly, I think how lucky I am that my family moved to Liberty Falls.

It's hard to believe that just yesterday I was missing Alaska and my old buds. That seems like years ago now.

I'm going to ask my dad if we can stop moving so much. I like it here.

No, I won't ask. I'll order him to stay. I'll shout, *Atten-shun, Sergeant!*

But I'll say it in a nicer way.

I remember the story that Eddie told me, and how Mr. Minks and Lady Minks looked at lots of places to live before picking Liberty Falls. Sometimes you find the perfect place to live immediately, but other times you have to move around until you find the perfect home.

I think Liberty Falls is the home for me. I don't want to be anywhere else. After all, the whole world is going to profit from the Minks Mystery Mansion, and I want to be right here to see it.

Although I think I've already profited from the Minks Mystery Mansion in all sorts of incredible ways already.

"What are you smiling about?" Eddie asks.

"I don't know. Everything, I guess."

ACKNOWLEDGMENTS

Thank you to Jody Corbett. Without your leadership and vision, the kids at Liberty Falls Elementary would never have ventured out of their school or even had a school to attend in the first place.

Thank you to everyone whose passions and talents helped make this book more book-ish, including gifted designer Yaffa Jaskoll, brilliant cover artist Mike Heath, remarkable illustrator Lissy Marlin, production editor extraordinaire Melissa Schirmer, eagle-eyed copy editor Rebekah Wallin—as well as Lauren Carr, Jana Haussman, Ann Marie Wong, Carolyn Scully—and everyone else at Scholastic who helps get my books get into the hands of readers.

Thank you to Kym, Veronica, Cherie, and Katie, critique partners and, at times, hand-holders.

Last, but not least, thank you to my family—Lauren, Emmy, and Madelyn, and Mom and Dad—who somehow put up with me.

ABOUT THE AUTHOR

Allan Woodrow loved going on field trips when he was in elementary school, although he never visited any place nearly as interesting as the Minks Mystery Mansion. The only thing he liked better than field trips was writing. Fortunately, he still gets to write.

Allan is the author of *Class Dismissed*, *Unschooled*, and *The Pet War*, as well as other books for young readers, many written under secret names. His writing also appears in the Scholastic anthology *Lucky Dog: Twelve Tales of Rescued Dogs*.

Allan currently lives near Chicago. He regularly visits schools and libraries, and sometimes is even invited to speak in them. For more about Allan and his books, visit his website at www.allanwoodrow.com.